To Marlon

a true friend that

I admire.

Tonya [illegible] Benton

Crying Out Loud

Tonya Phillips-Benton

AuthorHouse™
1663 Liberty Drive, Suite 200
Bloomington, IN 47403
www.authorhouse.com
Phone: 1-800-839-8640

First published by AuthorHouse 9/8/2008

ISBN: 978-1-4343-7521-6 (sc)

Printed in the United States of America
Bloomington, Indiana

This book is printed on acid-free paper.

Acknowledgements

Thanks to my higher power God for giving me life and the strength and courage to write and completing my destiny. to my husband Jessie Benton for support and the love he shares everday, and believing in me I love you so much.to my mom Vivian Smith thanks for caring and bringing me in this world my dad Roosevelt Smith. I wanna thank my dearest friend Bridget Pollard from Raleigh, North Carolina whom is always there when I need her. thanks for having the ambition , drive smarts, wit. you always will be my friend. to my closet friend Melissa Prophet for her consistant support and conversation you are an intelligent young woman stay positive. forever my friend. to my stepson Ramses Davis thanks for the love you show your Dad and me. to baby sis Ms Shanetta Phillips Warner for being strong I'm so proud of you. to my brother Gerry Phillips mr busy body for which is dedicated to his work. keep up the good work. you are a bright young man, I'm grateful to have a brother like you. thanks to china blue known as Valerie Duke for assisting me and helping me thank you for being a friend.I wanna thank Melissa Murray Howard, Gail Wooden , Sheila Roy, Angela Mcneill, August Pitt, Sheila Carper, Victoria Moses thank you guys for the support, laughs, fun. thanks to my sister Voneshia for assisting with my daughter. to my new friend Paula Clinton thanks for the rides, and being a friend. to Kenny Mccory thanks for the rides. a thanks to Ms Latrice Jenkins for coming up with a idea for my cover also knowing how law enforcement is done, the right way. a special thanks to Raymond Thompson, Rev. Charles Austin, Eric Poncho, Kenneth Tillman, Debra Jackson, Thanks to each and everyone who supported my journey.

Contents

Prelude

This story is how anyone can climb out of difficult situations with a little education, self-esteem and self-worth. Even when all hope is lost, having the courage and dignity to go on. This book is dedicated to all the self-motivated independent women of the world.

Chapter 1

Young Love

So it was the first day of school, September 7, 1985 and Cheryl was going into the eighth grade. She really didn't want to go, but her mama kept calling her from downstairs like she was across country or something. Cheryl was 15 years old and only starting the eighth grade.

Being tall made Cheryl feel sad at times. How embarrassing it was to be standing in the lunch line beside the other kids that was much shorter than she was. Failing the fourth grade twice really did make her fall way behind. She never talked much to the other kids, because they teased her a lot in elementary school, calling her bald headed and long bird legs. She couldn't do anything but cry. She didn't know how to fight back. She guessed that's why she would get upset. At times she would get angry and pick up chairs and try to hit some of the kids with them. Especially this one boy named Irvin who would call her names like Wolf-Man Jack. Cause her eyebrows were so thick and bushy. Her feelings was hurt, but she couldn't say or do anything cause she was scared of him. He said he would punch her if she told the teacher. So she would sit in the hallway and cry. It didn't make it any easier with the constant wetting herself. Her mother said she had a urinary tract infection when she was younger. She thought it probably came from when her godfather, a drug-addict touched her when she was ten years old. He got mad cause she wanted to play with her dolly baby; well that's what she called dolls when she was younger. Not knowing any better she didn't know what he was trying to do to her. As Cheryl grew older she understood what molestation meant.

It's now first period class and Cheryl was sitting in a daze while everybody was chitchatting about what they did over the summer. All she could do was sit and stare, because she had nothing to say about the summer. She did nothing but play with her sisters and brother outside in the messy grass. Play kick ball with the neighbors, which sometimes was boring cause they did not want her to play. Cheryl did not even know how to ride a bike. She couldn't jump rope, play hopscotch, or even play jacks. She felt useless when the other kids her age could do everything, even drive cars. This didn't matter to her if they drove. She did not want to learn how to drive anyway. As she was sitting in her seat waiting for the teacher to call her name for roll call the students starting laughing as soon as she called out Cheryl's name. She thought to herself "here I go again" it started in elementary and now in junior high school. Look at her hair! It's so short and bald one girl said. She got on Morton's clothes and Kinney shoes another girl said. She knew it bothered her but she couldn't let them get to her the way it used to.

Mrs. Lawrence scolded the girl for talking bad about Cheryl in the classroom. That's why she did not want to go to school cause she knew this was going to happen. It never seems to end. Cheryl wanted to get up and walk out of the classroom. Are you okay Cheryl said Mrs. Lawrence? Yes Cheryl said. I just wanna go home. With a slight grin Mrs. Lawrence said how come your hair is so short? Cheryl felt so embarrassed as Mrs. Lawrence walked around the room staring at her hair. Cheryl knew her hair was short but she couldn't help that. She kinda blamed her mama for the way her hair was. She kept putting relaxers and perms in her hair and it was just hard for it to grow back. When she got home from that terrible day she wanted to take her anger out on her mama, but it wasn't her mama's fault that those ignorant kids were bothering her.

The next day she told her mother she was having cramps, but her period was not for two more weeks and she knew that it wasn't going to work, not with her mother anyway. Cheryl was walking to school; all dressed up in her tight-fitting Gloria Vanderbilt jeans and her pink pullover sweater and penny loafers. She felt good the second day, cause she was more at ease, But when she was on her way to school, There was a guy following her home. As she turned around he began smiling. Cheryl was scared of what he might do to her,

When he got closer she started to walk faster what's wrong? He said.

"Leave me alone, I don't know you.

I'm not going to hurt you he said"

"How will I know that?"

I just wanna get to know you that's all baby.

My name is Darnell what's your name?

It's Cheryl.

That's a nice name. Please to meet you. He said. My mother said I couldn't have no boyfriend. I'm too young for that right now. How old are you, Cheryl? Well how old are you since you asked me my age Darnell? I'm 19 he said. I would have to ask my mother if I can talk to you. Girl don't you know everybody has a friend these days. But Cheryl said she was too young." I see right now I'm going to have to break you in. What's break' me in mean said Cheryl? So what's on your agenda this afternoon Darnell said? Nothing really, just gonna go home to do some homework. Homework Oh! Come on girl won't you hang out with me? Where she asked? I have to go home. My mother is going to worry.

Do you like go-go bands he said? What's go-go she asked? Its music he said laughing. Now that you mentioned it I heard that kind of music before and I don't like it much Cheryl said. Why? Cause it gives me headache she said. And I don't go out much. You get with me and that will change said Darnell. What makes you think I'm gonna like you? I can see it in your pretty brown eyes he said. Looks can be deceiving she replied. You know Let me have your phone number. Alright I'll give you my number, but only to talk. No problem, he said walking down the street with his funny-looking haircut and high-top adidas tennis shoes.

When Cheryl got home, a couple hours later the phone rang, and it was Darnell and she was waiting for him to call. After talking for a while, they decided to go to this place called the black hole where there were a lot of kids their age. Come on girl let's dance he said, but she didn't wanna dance. I can't dance she cried. I'll show you how, he said. Darnell wasn't shy at all but Cheryl was cause she had never been to a place like this before. So then we left the nightclub, Darnell started smirking, let's go to my place for a while, he said. I can't do that said Cheryl. My mother is going to get worried. You know what kills me about you Darnell said? What she said scared shaking not knowing what he was going to do to her. You always are worrying about what somebody says. Cheryl had to go home and Darnell said you're just stupid. Tears begin running down her face. What are you crying for? He said. Just leave me alone. Since all you do is call me stupid. Well go home stupid. How am I getting home she asked? I don't have any money. Here is $2.00 to catch the bus. So Cheryl went home.

As she was knocking on the door her Mama answered very angrily. Who is it, she said? It's me mama. What are you doing coming in here this late? It is after 12:00 am in the morning. I went out with Darnell. "Who in the hell is Darnell her mother said? A friend of mine Cheryl replied." "He took you where?" We went to a go-go party. I didn't tell you to go out, Well where did you meet him? I met him on my way home from school. How old is this nigger anyway. Cheryl said I don't know. You telling me you went out with somebody and he didn't tell you his age. We did not talk about that ma. Cheryl knew that Darnell told her how old he was but she knew that her mother wouldn't understand. You are only 15 years old. It's late, and you have school in the morning.

The next day as she was getting ready for school she noticed Darnell sitting on the front porch, as though he was waiting to walk her to school. All she needed was for her mama to be already fixing bacon and eggs, toast, and grits, for breakfast. Who is that on my front porch, that's Darnell. What the shit is he doing on my porch? He's waiting for me to walk me to school. I'm going out there to ask him what do he want said Cheryl's mother. Please ma, don't do that. This is my front porch I can do what I wanna do. This is where my husband and I pay bills. Daddy pay bills don't he ma. Are you getting smart? No, he looks like he's too old for you anyway. He's not old, how do you know? You don't even know how old he is. Go to schoolgirl. As Cheryl walked outside Darnell grabbed her by the hand. My mother said we should not be seeing each other. Your mother don't even know me. She guesses she feels like that I'm too young for a boyfriend. Well, I'll see you this evening. Okay.

When she got home from school the phone rang and mama answered it. It was Darnell. She asked, "What do you want with my daughter, she's too young for you." And then she passes me the telephone. Don't stay on long you have homework to do. What's wrong with your mother why is she so over protected? She's just worried that's all. You will have to understand her.

I don't have to understand nothing she needs to let you grow up and be a woman he said. I want to talk to you about something. This is bothering me. What is it he said? How old are you for real. It's just that you look older. I'm 19 he says .I wanna meet your mother and come over today. Hold on Darnell I will ask her. He wants to meet you mama. For what? I don't like that nigger. But you don't even know him. Were just friends. I don't care what you are I don't want him in here. Ma you haven't met him yet. Give him a chance. I'll be over there in 2 hours. My mother said she don't want to meet you. I'll handle that. And she hung up the phone, Ma he's just coming over to watch T.V and talk and maybe listen to the stereo. Don't keep arguing with me I'm your mother you ain't mine. She said shouting. That nigger just want some pussy anyway. Ma he never got fresh with me I was only telling you he's coming over. We already discussed this Cheryl so shut your freakin mouth. There was a knock at the door so she went to open it. It was Darnell. He came in and sat down on the sofa. Staring at me with a strange look on his face as though he could eat me up. Why arc you staring at me like that? But then Mama came out of the kitchen with a look of hatred on her face. Hi you doing miss, he said. Please, she said. Cheryl didn't I tell you I don't want that nigger in here you're hardheaded. Why is your mother so damn mean he said? She's acting that way cause I'm young said Cheryl. Mother then said, me and Roy are going up to Ann and Earl's house and when we get back your company better be gone. So now that your mother and father gone, what's up Darnell said? She will be back soon Cheryl said. They just went up there to drink some beer. Cheryl went to the bathroom and when she came out Darnell was standing on the steps.

What are you doing up here my mother and father will be coming back soon and if they see you up here I'm going to be in a lot of trouble. Shut up and stop acting like a little girl and grow up and act like a woman he said in a rage. Cheryl went into her room to get a cassette tape she's been wanting to hear. Go back downstairs please? As she turned around he grabbed and kissed her. What are you doing? What the fuck I'm doing he said. Get your young ass in this bed. And give me some of this good pussy. What are you doing she yelled and then he slid his penis inside her vagina. She knew this was rape but she didn't want to accuse him of rape. I was just starting to like him. As I shouted out mama's name he slapped me in the face shouting Girl shut up, your mother ain't here. When Cheryl got up from the bed she was bleeding from her vagina. She had been raped. I told him no go back downstairs before her mother comes back but he insisted on having sex with her. Cheryl then changed her clothes and put on some sweat pants. When she went downstairs he was sitting there smiling with a smirk on his face. Cheryl said, I think you better leave. I'm bleeding from my vagina and you're sitting here smiling. So what you bleeding he said, what's the big fuckin big deal? So you're telling me you don't care about me or how I feel, did you know I was a virgin? You ain't no virgin girl, who do you think you're fooling? What am I going to tell going to tell my mother? Just tell her I banged you he said. How can you be at ease with this situation? I'm going to be in a lot of trouble when she gets back home. Her sister came downstairs and said you're a whore. She's my whore Darnell he said. Why are you calling me a whore? Your sister said it first doesn't that matter. Neither one of you had no business saying it. When my mother comes through the door, she's going to get suspicious about us. Darnell I'm scared, scared of what he said? You forced yourself on me .How did I force myself on you? I told you no Cheryl cried. And you kept fighting with me insisting on having sex.

My mom went upstairs and my father went downstairs to talk to Darnell and drank some beer. What are these bloody ass underwear doing in the bathroom. Cheryl It's not time for your menstrual period yet, she said. In a rage. What happen in here while we were gone? Nothing we just talking. Look like something went on here you ask me. Something did go on Ma, Darnell and Cheryl was upstairs having sex." What! She said ". Mind your own business Nicole. I think she should know about your nasty boyfriend. You have nothing to do with this, but I do. Mama said, How old are you man don't you think you're too old for my daughter. I'm 19 years old. You don't look like it. Look more like 29 why are you worrying about my age? I told you my age miss so let it go. He said. At that time I ask Darnell to leave before mama did. You can get out. Getting smart in my house where me and my husband pay rent at. Darnell just leave she don't want any trouble. You stupid little girl, when you grow up and be a woman give me a call okay. And he left so she went upstairs to her dreary looking bedroom. She felt sad the whole day. I didn't feel like talking to anyone.

The next day he called me and we talked. Listen I like you and want to see you again. I don't know about that right now. What you mean you don't know. Well you're with me for life so face up to it. And besides my ma was very upset about what happened. If she would mind her business everything will be all right. I'm her daughter she's gonna be concerned. She didn't want any commotion that's why she asked you to leave. When are you coming over my house so we can really make love he said? Is that all you think about is having sex with me. Because if sex is all you have on your mind then we can't see each other. No I like you baby give me a chance. We do have something to talk about she said, go ahead. Your real age. You stupid. Act like a woman and make your own decisions and stop listening about your mother. I'm only 15 how can I make my own decisions? And I'm living with my parents. Get your own apartment he told Cheryl. I can't, I don't have a job she said. Then get one all you need is a work permit. My mother is not going to let me work. Your mother! I'm sick of hearing about your mother. That's the point; I'm trying to make you become a woman stupid ass. I'm tired of you calling me stupid. I'm getting away from you. If you do you're dead bitch. All you can do is make me feel bad. Then grow up and do what you suppose to do.

The next day Cheryl was so upset and Darnell came walking down the street drunk with big bottle of beer in his hand, staggering along the sidewalk. Come here girl, he said slurring. What do you want? I don't want to be bothered with you. Cheryl's mother came outside and said look nigger leave my daughter alone. After that she did not hear or see Darnell for 2 weeks, she began to worry where he was. Cheryl stared out her dirty windows everyday wondering if she would ever see him again. Even though, he called her names most of the time she really liked him as a person.

When she got to school her classmate Dana told her something that she did not want to hear at the time. Are you fooling around with Darnell she asked? Yes, but we're just friends. You need to leave him alone. Why? Are you involved with him? No I'm not she said. He lives with a woman. Cheryl said, I don't believe that. You just want him for yourself. Don't believe me, I'll take you on the road where he lives with this brother and you can see it for yourself. When school was out she really wanted to know if Dana was telling her the truth. But she didn't know where to look for him. So she had to wait until Dana come out of the school building. She really did not know how she knew about her and Darnell. As Dana came out of the school building she asked her where to go. Wait for me Cheryl and I'll take there. Okay she said. This is a bad idea she thought but I wanted to know.

On the way to Everett Rd which was not far from the high school it was the second house from the end of the alley. The next day Cheryl was running late to school so that she can see if Darnell lives there. She was afraid of knocking at the door but she did. And sure enough he was in the window where he was standing in the window flashing his naked body in the window. Whatcha doing around here? Cheryl said where have you been I have been worried about you? Your mother made it clear to me that she did not want me to see you. You still should have called me. Are you living with a woman? That's my aunt Brenda and why are you standing in the window exposing yourself to people, do you care? Just go home and I'll call you later. Matter fact; get your ass to school.

School was just let out. As Cheryl walked away a lady came out with a tan raggedy terry-cloth robe on. Who are you? The woman asked. I'm a friend of Darnell's. I'm his woman and you can get away from my house. Darnell I thought you told me she was your aunt. She is. It don't seem that way to me. So Cheryl went home and there was no calls from him until next week. What's up he said as I picked up the phone? You have who you want. How many times I'm going tell you she's my aunt. She said different. Alright I lived with her but she threw my clothes out anyway. Why did you lie about it in the first place? Cause it's not your business. Plus we had a fight. About what? You're mighty noisy. A couple hours later we had sex at this cheap tourist home on Michigan Ave. She didn't feel comfortable having sex with Darnell cause of the first time she had sex when she said no to him, actually he raped her and she knew he did but why would she get the police involved when she care about him so much. Cheryl knew if she told her mama that he forced his self on her she would be angry right now, she knows we had sex but she can't tell her face to face.

Weeks went past and she started to feel nauseas and vomiting. Mama went to the drug store to get a pregnancy test. Now Cheryl became nervous because she didn't know anything about being pregnant. An hour later the test was yes. Cheryl started to get scared.

She then told her mama that she don't want to go to school today, cause she wasn't feeling well but she insisted that she go since she had a test today. As she was walking across the bridge from school, she spotted Darnell and Raven holding hands together as though they belong together, but she knew he belong to her. "What is this" girl go home he said. Cheryl wasn't going anywhere until she found out why Darnell was walking down the street with her. Her classmate of all people. If you would go home and do your homework you'll be all right. He said. "Look if you want her you can have her. Bitch who do you think you're talking to in that tone. He said. Well Raven did you know he got me pregnant. Got who pregnant? Me bitch you trippin. Now he was getting mad cause she embarrassed him in front of that Raven. So me and Darnell is going to smoke some marijuana together and fuck Raven said. She threw the leather gloves he gave her on the ground, which he found them inside a trash bin. And then gave them to her in which she appreciated them but now since she saw him with Raven she had no use for them. She thought, maybe it was a mistake for Darnell and her to see each other. What's wrong with her following you as though ya'll married? Don't pay her any attention she's crazy, we'll see who's crazy when I have the baby. Do what you have to do. Let's go Raven she's a crazy bitch and slow.

When she got home she couldn't wait to call him at his sister's house, which there was where he was staying. Hello she answered. Can I speak to Darnell? No you can't I'm fucking him right now. And she hung up the phone. Cheryl then calls again to speak to Darnell.

This time he answered laughing as he lifted the phone. Darnell why did you let Raven answer your telephone saying that to me? Cause she felt like it. Goodbye and don't call me anymore. Cheryl was crying so bad she couldn't catch her breath. What's wrong with you mama asked. I saw Darnell walking down the street with Raven. Who's Raven? A girl in my class. Ain't no sense you getting yourself all upset about it. She said. But I'm pregnant with his baby mama. Can I go over there? For what child? Shit let the nigger go. We are behind you on this 100% even though I'm disappointed Cheryl's mother said. You can't depend on a black ass nigger no way. Cheryl won't be satisfied until she catches a cab to his house. She then pick up the phone and called a cab to 4370 Stanford Rd.

As me and mama got out the cab he answered who it is. He then opens the door smiling. You telling me you and mother came all the way over here in 20-degree weather. As she walked in she didn't see Raven but she notice the bed all messed up with the sheets dirty and cigarette butts and empty beer bottles and a mirror with slices of divided powder on it. She did not know what they were doing with that I really wanted to find out she then asked mama if she was ready to go. And she was. Listen Darnell I don't approve of you and Cheryl dating. And she's pregnant with your kid I hope you live up to your responsibility. She don't even know if it's mine. The baby is yours. We'll see he said. You can't be pregnant with my kid because I had a vasectomy. Well you are the only one I've been sleeping with, anyway I haven't went to doctor's office yet to be sure but I took a test. So I will call you tomorrow and let you know when my appointment is, you don't have to call me and tell nothing he said.

Cheryl called the doctor's and they told her to come in next week on Tuesday at 10:00 in the morning. She went in that day. Yes, I'm here to see Dr. Brown for an examination. Before Cheryl could say anything Mama said she needs to take a pregnancy test. Now what's the problem with you? Dr. Brown said. Well I've been feeling a little nausea and vomiting, I also been irritated down in my vagina. Sounds like you need a pregnancy test and a culture, what's a culture. A culture is a test we use to detect any signs of venereal diseases. Go to the room and get undressed and the nurse will be in shortly. Hours later Dr. Brown came in after the exam and said I was infected with Trichomoniasis and Chlamydial venereal disease. Where does this comes from. Well Cheryl it comes from sexual contact. So I'm going to give you some prescriptions to treat it with. Cheryl and her mother left the doctor's office and Cheryl noticed the look on her mother's face. She knew she was angry that she was pregnant and infected with this disease, which she knew Darnell transmitted to her, which she didn't deserve. But there was nothing she could do about it.

When she got home she called a friend of hers named Pebbles. Hey girl, what's up? Nothing. You sound sad what's wrong with you. I went to the doctor's office today. What did they say? I'm 2 months pregnant and contracted a venereal disease. So you caught it from Darnell I suppose? Yes where else would I get it from? You should get rid of him he's no good for you. I can't. I love him. He's my first love. You know nothing about love. You're only 15 years old. Have you told him yet? Yes, but mama got a test from the drug store but we wanted to be sure that I really am. Now I really know. I don't know what to do. Mama said she's going to help me. You're not getting an abortion. No. Girl I feel sorry for you. Why? You are pregnant with your first baby. Your mother is going to beat your ass if she finds out you're pregnant. For your information she already knows I'm pregnant. Listen Pebbles let me worry about this problem. Cheryl just doesn't know how she's going to make it with a baby. Have you talked to Darnell lately? No I haven't. Look Pebbles I will talk to you later I have some things to do. Don't get mad at me because your ignorant boyfriend left you pregnant and lonely. Goodbye Pebbles I have to go.

The next day came no calls and no visits from Darnell. She heard Mama coming upstairs. What's wrong with you been sitting in this room the whole weekend there's something bothering you. No Cheryl said feeling miserable because she hasn't heard from Darnell. Monday came and she wasn't feeling well. So she asked mama can she stay home from school today, but she knew she was not going to say yes considering she wants all her kids to get an education. No you can't stay home hussy. Get your ass up and go to school. So she went to school and as she was walking across the bridge Darnell was sitting on a log. Where have you been I have been worried about you? For what? What do you mean for what? I've been playing it cool. I went to the doctor and they said I'm pregnant and I have a venereal disease. You ain't get it from me and how do you know I'm the father. I was a virgin when I met you. How do I know that? I'll talk to you later he said sounding angry. After he walked away Cheryl didn't even feel like going to school so she went towards the park to do some thinking at that time she felt like diving into the water. But she knew that wouldn't be right. So she waited until around 3:00 to go home if she knew she was to go home now mama would be upset. So she called Pebbles. To tell her, she ran into Darnell. Hello she said. Hi Pebbles what it is. I just called to talk to you. I know you Cheryl; it's about that no good boyfriend of yours. But Pebbles you don't understand I really care about Darnell. Well that's your dumbness. Have you heard from him lately? Yes, I saw him sitting on a log on my way to school today. What did he say about the baby? He thinks that I'm lying. Don't that tell you something she said? Tell me what. He don't want you He's just using you for your body. Look Pebbles he loves me and I love him. He'll call me and realize that he was wrong about this. Why are you sounding so sad Cheryl, it's the truth so face it. The next couple of hours later Darnell called and said he would destroy her reputation if she had the baby. We're both responsible she said as she put down the telephone. Get a job and be a woman still living with your mother he said. Get a job and stop being so damn lazy? How can you tell me to get a job when you don't have one? And stop selling drugs. Get a life bitch and finish school. He said and hung up the phone. Cheryl then called back. Hello, he said answering the phone. Darnell are you trying to break up with me to get out of your responsibility of our child. No I'm not. I can do what ever I want to do. We ain't married and never will be. I just want to know if you're gonna take care of our baby. Because I can take care of my baby all by myself. How when you can't even take care of your damn self. Still leaning on your mother and father for help. You run to your mother every time we disagree on something. Just like a little girl. Goodbye let me know when you have this baby, if it's mine.

It's been three months since Cheryl heard from Darnell. Cheryl's 16th birthday came and she's now seven months pregnant and still has not heard from him. It's now getting closer to her due date. And she wanted him there for the baby, but she knew he was gone, and wouldn't come back to her. The next day some water was running down my legs. Mama I need your help. What is it? Some water is running from my vagina. Your water broke child. It's time for you to have the baby. I can't go right now. What do you mean you can't go? It ain't nothing but that nigga you're running after cause you to go in labor early. Darnell didn't do this. Look we'll discuss that later. I'm calling the ambulance. As the ambulance pulled up in front of the run-down projects where Cheryl lived, neighbors were standing outside as though they saw a ghost or something. But then she felt shamed considering I'm still young and having a baby at my age. But it was too late for sorrow, when we arrived at the hospital the nurse lifted me out of the wheel chair. Okay, let's get you into a gown and lay back. The doctor will be in a minute to give you an exam. An hour later they examined her and told her she had an infection which was called gonorrhea and that can cause some damages to the baby. And that she has a high-risk pregnancy. Is this your first baby mam?

Yes she said shivering. Is that why you're so nervous the nurse said? Where's her mother? She needs to be with her right now. Cheryl's Mama was then paged. The doctor came back in the room to tell Cheryl that he would have to induce her labor. Mama walked in the room wandering what they were going to do. Cheryl said, Mama the nurse said they were going to induce my labor. They have to Cheryl her mother said. But I have been in here for 9 hours. This is your first child so you have to be patient. Mama then left the room to go outside to light a cigarette. As she was pushing herself back up into the bed. She was actually really getting inpatient with the itching and the burning sensation from her vagina.

The nurse came back into her room saying she would need to get a needle. A needle for what? Well it's called an epidural that's what the doctor uses for inducing labor. She started paining as though she was coming on her menstrual period. The pain was unbearable by now. She began to yell as loud as she could. Mama rushed through the labor room what's wrong with you child I heard you all the way down the hallway. Chcryl was really scared to have a baby. But mama was there to give her support. 4 hours later Cheryl's son was born at 6:31 pm on August 12, 1986. As the nurse was wheeling her in the wheelchair she noticed the expression on mama's face she kinda felt disappointed that she got pregnant and she also felt proud of her first grandchild. Ma I feel depressed said Cheryl. For what she said. Because of the stupid-ass man of yours ain't here? Yes she thought Darnell would be here. Look don't worry about him what you need to do is concentrate on your newborn son and forget about Darnell. But she couldn't. He's the father and it's obvious he don't give a shit about you or your son. He's probably hanging out with his friends. He doesn't even know you had his child. Well, I'm going home kid. If you need me call but I'll be back tomorrow. Okay I'll see you tomorrow said Cheryl. As she gently walked her mama to the end of the hospital hallway to see that she gets on the elevator. Darnell was coming off the elevator, as mama was getting on; it's about time you showed up. Mama said. Darnell where have you been I have been worried. Taking care of my business. You don't have to get smart I just ask you a question. You asking me questions have you brushed your teeth today? "He said. Have you stopped selling drugs? What did you say bitch? He then punched her in the face with his fist. He then hit her and she fell to the floor holding her stomach. As she was reaching for something to hold on to. The hospital staff went to get the police officers is there a problem young lady. Yes my boyfriend hit me. Is this true sir? Yeh! I seen the whole thing, said a woman who was standing in the hall. She said okay mam we want to hear it from him. Did you assault this young lady sir? Yeh! Cause of her running her damn mouth. You will have to leave the hospital. I wanna see my son. Or do you want to go to jail tonight. Darnell started to get physical with police and then he was hauled off to jail. For resisting arrest. At that time she did not care because of what he did to her here she just gave birth to our son and he hits me for nothing. The nurse then entered my room with my son as I was getting myself out of that small bed they had me lying in for 2 days.

I couldn't wait to hold him and feed him but I got sad because Darnell was not here to see his son. The next day he came back to the hospital. Where's my son he said. With liquor on his breath smelling bad his clothes were dirty, and shoes did not have shoe strings in them by the way he looked I could tell he was using drugs instead of selling them. I wanna know where my son is. He's getting some tests done. What kind of tests he had yellow jaundice in his blood. What the fuck is jaundice? It comes from an infection in the blood can he get, how in the fuck did he get that shit. Maybe it came from all those venereal diseases you gave me. Bitch! I did not give you a damn thing so you need to stop accusing me of your nasty ass ways. After that heated argument we had. I knew that it was time to let him go. All with him using drugs now I knew the relationship would not work anyway, the next day I was leaving the hospital with my son. I was getting depressed the nurse told me I was going to be feeling this kind of symptom called post-partum depression but I'm feeling sad because of the argument we had and I knew I going to have to take care of my child by self. The next day he showed up at the house the same way but now he looked worse. I couldn't understand why he don't change his clothes and take a bath when I first met him he was such a clean-cut guy. Hey he said as he walked in the front door smelling bad as he looked. Where's my son. He's taking a nap wake his little ass up. You can get outta here nigga with kind of language mama said. Can I talk to Cheryl he said. Cheryl lets go outside and talk. Talk about what. Will you marry me? I'm too young to get married and mama ain't gonna approve anyway.

There you go again not being a woman like I told you to be. We can move together. Darnell I can do that. Well here's an engagement ring. When she went to tell her mama she got really hostile but she knew she wasn't going to approve of this, but then she got upset when mama told Darnell to leave. If you going to take his side then both of ya'll mutherfuckers can leave and my grandson can stay here with me and Roosevelt. So then Cheryl threw the stereo out from the entertainment shelf. She felt angry. She then went to her room to pack up her and the baby's things. Darnell was sitting outside waiting. He flagged down a cab. She did not know where she was going until the cab pulled up in front of a rooming house. Where people was standing outside drinking beer and others were nodding as though they were falling asleep but then she knew that was drugs that was making them react that way. Kids were yelling and crying. Some of them were getting whippings from their drug-addicted mothers. The building we went in smelled like urine and defecation, needles, beer bottles, used pampers, writings on the wall of the building.

Now Cheryl was feeling bad for leaving the house and leaving her family to come to a disgusting place such as this. All her mama did for her and she left to come here with him. Knowing she need to go home with her family. The way Darnell been acting she should not be here anyway. But she would feel guilty going back now. Brian starting crying and he only had 2 bottles Darnell did not have any money to get him any infant formula and either did Cheryl. Days and days were going by and he ran out of diapers. He needs some pampers she said. Look cut up this sheet and put it on his ass. He'll be all right. I can't use this. Shut up bitch. And then slapped her and turned her face red. Don't you see I'm trying to get high don't disturb me anymore or I'm going to put my foot up in your ass. It's been nearly 4 months and they were just getting by with baby formula and diapers. Darnell had to borrow money so that they could eat. But she did not eat much because he just get baby formula and diapers for Brian but the baby needed it and when he did get food he would eat and give her what he did not finish. Which made her feel bad, after he would eat some chicken he would give her practically the bones but she had no other choice but to eat it, since she had nothing else to eat.

A couple of weeks went by and her mama got worried and started calling the police, but it was her mothers idea for Cheryl to leave and besides, Brian was still a infant when they left home. The next day they all left Cheryl just couldn't put with no more of this drug-infested building and Darnell with his dope –dealing and abusing drugs. When Cheryl got home her mama was overwhelmed when her and the baby got there. Hours later Darnell showed up at the front door saying he was sorry for taking Cheryl and the baby away like that. Yeh! Mama said. Cheryl said you had her and my grandson in some low- down roach infested apartment building. "Yes I did. "He said" well do me a favor get the hell away from my door and away from daughter and grandson. All right if that's the way you want it. You don't have anything to do with this he said shouting at mama. From that heated argument her mama didn't like Darnell anymore. The next day he returned saying he needed to talk to Cheryl, but she had to meet him outside. There's something I need to talk to you about." What is it Cheryl asked? I've been seeing someone else Darnell said. Who? She's a nurse and I care about her.

From the way he said it. Cheryl's heart felt like it was in her stomach. Why are you telling me this now? Cause you need to know and I love her. I thought you loved me Cheryl said. You thought wrong. Did I ever tell you I loved you? "No" but I thought you did. Darnell you can't leave me and the baby like this, I'll take care of my son but I'm sick of you and your damn mother. I told you in the beginning I only wanted sex from you said Darnell. If you leave me for that woman you never see our baby ever again Cheryl said. Bitch! "You crazy" he yelled. Darnell go on to your new woman since you love her so much she said. If you think you are going to keep me from my son you're fuckin crazy. Well I'm not going to ever let you see him again, when Cheryl turned around he hit her and she fell to the floor. He then said stay in child's place and keep your fuckin mouth shut, before I hit your stupid ass again. "You dumb ass bitch". Cheryl was so embarrassed; she couldn't go back inside, because her mama would have got upset so she stayed out there sitting in the grass.

When she did go inside mama "shouted "what happen to you" Darnell hit me because I said he couldn't see the baby anymore. That egotistical bastard I should have got his ass arrested for statutory –rape you wasn't but 15 he is 25 years old. I'm calling the police on his ass. Please ma don't do that he'll be mad if I get him locked up. I don't give a shit what he gets mad at. After all the confusion, Darnell had a nerve to show with his new girlfriend as they enter the door Cheryl's heart felt like it dropped in inside her stomach, What do you want Darnell, said Cheryl's mother haven't you caused enough trouble? What trouble, I'm here to see my son and I'm taking my him. You can't take my grandson outta here. Is that your sister Cheryl's daddy asked "No that's my woman this is my new baby her name is Thomasine. You and your woman get the hell out of my apartment. You ain't taking my grandson nowhere, I didn't come here for no trouble I just want my son Darnell said. Cheryl just went to her bedroom to avoid all the arguing that was going on. She couldn't stand to see him and that lady standing there as though nothing was going on. She then went to the bathroom to wipe the tears from her eyes, when she came out Darnell and Thomasine was still there waiting for her to give them the baby, are you going to let me take my son out or not, cause if you ain't then I'll leave, and I will be coming back tomorrow. Before he would have time to come back Cheryl was so hurt over to Darnell's new woman and apartment she lit his car on fire. Cheryl knew that wasn't the right thing to do, but shc could not stand to see him come over her house with another woman and then rub it in her face. Cheryl learned a lesson about getting involved with someone just doesn't care much about their self or the love of anybody else.

Chapter 2

Infidelity

The school year was approaching, and Cheryl decided to go back to school since Brian was turning 2 years old now, it was a little complicated with her trying to get up again and getting ready for school, but her mother baby sat Brian while she continued her education. Cheryl actually went back to high school for only a couple of months until she was gang-raped by two men in their mid- thirties, that was devastating for her. She never told her mother about it until after she was released form D. C. General hospital from torn tissues in her vagina, Cheryl couldn't go back to the house so she stayed away for three days, when she did go home her mama was worried about where she was, Cheryl knew she should have told her mama but she just couldn't tell her she was raped by two men. She didn't even tell the police that.

As she was sitting in her room her mama kept interrogating her on where she had been. "Where have you been and why haven't you been to school? Cheryl said she was too old to be in the 10th grade whatcha you mean you too old her mamma said. I'm 17 going on 18 years old. Poobie told her about the job corps center in S.W. So Cheryl was going there to finish her education and get her diploma. Two weeks later she had enrolled in Job Corps center, She had to walk 12 blocks to catch the campus bus which wasn't hard since she needed her education, Cheryl first day was actually ok, She met all the teachers whose classes she would be attending, when she got home she told the rest of the family that she enjoyed her first day at job corps, but somehow she couldn't really concentrate on what she was doing, because of the rape had her in a terrible state of mind, but she knew she had to continue going since she had already enrolled there. As days and weeks went by she met a lot of new people besides Poobie since she already knew her anyway. One girl Cheryl met was Lynn they both were studying word processing they started talking about how they both enjoyed the class together, they exchanged phone numbers so they could discuss the course they were taking, Lynn said she liked going to clubs, cabarets, a couple of weeks later they started going to this place called the Brine Manor.

It was a spot where they play bingo, but at times they would hold dances there, one night Cheryl was just sitting in her room bored watching T. V. What she normally do on a Saturday night since she didn't have a boyfriend anymore, the phone rang and it was Lynn are you going out tonight? Going out where? Cheryl asks.

Me and my mother are giving a disco tonight at Byrne Manor, are you going? Cheryl said Yes I'll go sounding excited, so she got dressed up in a short leather- mini-skirt and a silk lacy blouse with her elegant sheer panty hose and her high-heel black pumps, and besides after her and Darnell broke up was time for her to go out, and meet a new set of people. She was bored all the time, just sitting around the house and going to school.

It was now going on 10:00pm and Lynn still hasn't showed up. She wasn't getting impatient, she kept looking out of the window to see if she was coming, a couple of minutes later Lynn and her mother Mrs. Paula pulled up in a red Toyota Camry so Cheryl jumped in the back seat and off they went to the disco well it's about time Cheryl said, I've been waiting for two hours, well I'm here now so stop nagging, said Lynn. Cheryl said I can't wait until we get there I love to dance I've never been out to a disco before, I 'm so tired of being home all the time.

By the look on Lynn and Mrs. Paula's face she could tell they wanted her to shut-up which she did when we arrived at the disco. The place looked crowed as they walked in the door. Lynn said Come on, Cheryl stop acting so shy we're going to have a good time girl. Cheryl said I know it's just that people are staring at me, they was staring, as though she was a movie star or something entering a ballroom. Well let them look, said Lynn. I'm here to have a good time as the night went on Cheryl got really relaxed especially when the DJ played "she's a bad mama jam " by Carl Carlton " the song was old, but she liked it because it reminded her of herself. Cheryl thought, I'm going to get up and dance, then

Lynn said and stop being so shy, as Cheryl started to dance she felt as though nobody wanted to dance with her so she then left the dance floor to go over to the bar to get a drink. Which this would be the first time she wanted to drink but then she decided not to drink, because she didn't want her mama to know she had been drinking alcohol. She then went to sit down and got up again and went back to the bar and the bartender asked her what would you like to drink miss, give me a glass of gin and juice. Here you go he said enjoy your night with a smile, Cheryl went back to her seat nodding her head to the music, girl you betta get up and dance Lynn said, I'm going to dance I didn't come to this disco to just sit and look stupid. Cheryl then was feeling a little tipsy she got back on the dance floor; she stayed a little longer this time. Then a guy from nowhere came over and started dancing with her. She knew she was having fun. What's your name he said staring down at her long legs, which was scared, from running from those men that brutally raped her, but she guess in his mind her legs looked good according to the way he was looking at them. My name is Cheryl and what's yours she said smiled, its Ronnie he said.

They started dancing and they danced the night away, so what made you come out tonight, I needed to get out she said. I find you very pretty, thank you she said with a sigh. Do you come out often? Not really, my friend Lynn told me about a disco she and mother were giving so I decided to go. Do you go out often she asks, sometimes but I would rather stay at home. What you do for a living? Nothing right but go to school and stay at home with my son. How old is your son, one and a half years old. Are you still with the father? No I'm not we had a disagreement he left me for a much older woman? Is it possible we can go out sometime? Cheryl really couldn't answer him at that time knowing she was raped she was still kinda shaken up from this situation and she didn't want to get involved in another relationship.

Being still so young, right now she was taking her time getting herself back into another relationship she said to him. Would you like another drink he said? Sure, as he walked over to the bar, she stood there watching him with a suspicious look on her face, thinking to herself would he be worth my time or would he be a change in my life, but then again he might be another ass-hole, like Darnell so he came back over to the table where she was sitting. Did you miss me? Not really she said laughing I'm just kidding Ronnie; you should see the look on your face. What look? You have that look of disgust, are you okay she asked yeh! I'm a little tipsy off of this drink that's all. May I ask what is it, Hennessy and coke. Do you know what time this disco is over? In another half an hour, why are you in such a rush, I said, sounding concern is there someone you need to get home to? No he said in a trembling voice, it's just that it's getting late and I'm not the kinda man that stays out late, and I'm here with my some of my friends, And they are ready to leave. So maybe I'll see you another time, would I be coming on too strong if I ask if you and I can go somewhere to be alone? She said I thought you're ready to go home? After we go somewhere to talk. To answer your question, yes I think you would be coming on too strong Cheryl said. I'm not that kind of girl that would leave with a man I just met, and plus Lynn would be wondering where I'm at. I apologize for my actions, okay here's my pager number. Will you call me sometimes? Sure I will call you tomorrow, bye bye. Cheryl went back to the table and something was bothering her, why didn't he give her his home telephone, maybe his phone was cut off. She thought I'd find out when I talk to him on tomorrow.

After the last song went off which was chuck brown Bustin loose the DJ announced that the disco was now closing and the lights came on. Is your friend gone Lynn said? What's wrong with his head, and she started to laugh I don't know it might be cysts he have, I wanted to ask him that but I did not want to get personal, but I'm not worrying about that he seems like a nice guy, don't fall in love yet, she said. I'm not I learned my lesson before, did he give you his number, no, but he gave me his pager number, Girl That man is married, I don't think so, let's not start assuming, just yet, maybe he don't have a number, didn't you learn something from that mother fucker you just got away from? Yes, well the next time you see him ask him for his home number. Lynn what if he is married what should I do? Dump his sorry ass, she said. I don't want to dump him I like him already. Are you ready to go Cheryl? Lynn asked, yes I'm ready.

She thinking about what Lynn said about him being married as people were getting out of their seats, and walking towards the front door. Cheryl sat there wishing she left with Ronnie, but what would every one think if she did, I am a grown woman almost she thought, and I can do what I want to do, as long as I respect myself. She wondered if Ronnie would have respected her if she taken off with him not knowing what he would do to her. I could have been raped or even killed for that matter she thought; he probably thought I was some slut or something. So I'll wait until it's the right time whole time they were riding home she thought about it. Cheryl had Ronnie on her mind and they had just met when she got home she was restless and couldn't sleep she went downstairs to get a glass of milk. She supposed what Lynn said about Ronnie bothered her a bit. But she couldn't let that bother her she deserve to be happy just like everybody else, but then she was still learning how to deal with being in a relationship the next day Ronnie and Cheryl talked over the phone for at least two hours "Ronnie its something I need to ask you what is that he said sounding so sweet, I would like a honest answer, okay what is it? Is there a reason you didn't give me your phone number at home? No there's any reason. Well, why didn't you give it to me then, I gave you my pager number I know Ronnie it's just that when I call you I want to talk to you instead, of waiting until you call me back. At least you'll be talking to me listen let's not ruin a good moment okay, what good moment. I deserve an answer Ronnie I just don't think it's the right time yet he says. Are we still on for tomorrow? Yes I would love to go with you. Well I'll see you tomorrow and they hung up.

The next day Ronnie pulled up in front of the door in a blue Volvo looking somewhat scared when he got out of the car, she guesses he was staring like that because of where she lived. And you look lovely today thank you she said where did you get that beautiful dress from? I bought if from Marianne's. What's that? It's a women's clothing store. As time goes on we'll be shopping there he said. "Oh really, I like to shop Maybe we will be going shopping in our spare time what are some of the things you enjoy doing? I like to dance, go bowling, and go out to dinner. Sounds like hobbies I enjoy as well, so when they arrived at the restaurant Cheryl is thinking they were going to a elegant restaurant he pulls up in front of Denny's maybe I'm not good enough to be taken to Red lobster's or any other nice place to dine she thought. She thought to herself of course, when they went inside to be seated. Ronnie is chewing gum so loud other people had to turn around and look. Ronnie you're chewing that gum a little loud, she told him 'oh " I'm sorry he said still chopping away, since we're in the restaurant she thinks it's a good time to ask him why can't he give her his home number.

As we were waiting on our meal Ronnie may I ask you a question? Yes what it is dear, are you married he then cranked a smile, I'm not smiling Ronnie. This is serious all right you want the truth. Yes I do. Yes I am a marricd man her heart started to pound as he said yes why didn't you tell me in the beginning? Because it wasn't none of your business. What do you mean? I don't like going out with married men. So are saying you don't want to see me anymore? I didn't say that it's just that I would not get enough of your time and it's not right in god's eye that's all. Trust me we'll get to see each other a lot. How much? Damn it, Cheryl you're making a mountain out of a mold hill. Ronnie you don't have to scream I just ask you a question. I just wanna know what I'm getting myself into. Look Ronnie I think if we are going to seeing each other we should get to know each other better. I agree with you. Then if you agree with me, then I don't understand why it's such a secret that you're a married man. You didn't have a problem asking me to spend the night with you. I'm glad you said no. I would have lost all respect for you. I'm not that kind of girl that would eagerly go with a man the first night anyway.

It was getting late and I knew I needed to get home to my son. I really enjoyed myself Ronnie she told him. Before Cheryl got to the front door, she could smell the aroma coming from the kitchen mama you always cook us good meals, anyway is there any more dinner left? As she was taking off her clothes, trying to butter her up it's in the oven kid, mama shouted out. I'm surprised she didn't ask me why am I coming in here so late but until she does I'm going upstairs to take me a shower she thought. She went downstairs to eat her dinner mama prepared fried chicken, macaroni /cheese, collard greens, and big jug of cherry Kool-Aid ma the food was good well I'm going to bed she said. Everybody was asleep even Brian, Standing there watching him sleep made me think of Darnell, but that's all over now, and now she can move on to a new life and a happy one that she attend to have with Ronnie. Thinking of Ronnie in two days it will be Valentines Day and mama's birthday, what a celebration this is gonna be, knowing that I will be getting gifts from Ronnie. But I'm not going to get my hopes up so high the only thing I can do is wish he would pick me up something. A couple hours later there was a knock at the door looking in the peep-hole through the front door it was Ronnie, which she was hoping it was him, standing there with a bouquet of flowers. These are for you beautiful he said. Thank you she said smiling and happy Valentines Day to you. What's on your agenda for today he asks? Nothing just waiting here for you she said. I'm sorry I can't stay I gotta make a run. Why not? Okay I'll walk you out to your car, when she walked Ronnie out in the back seat of the car there was a dozen of roses and a box of shoes from Hecht's. I see you have some roses for me. Yeh those are not for you those are for my wife. Excuse me I didn't know. Well. You should know. Come on Cheryl get serious don't you think if those roses were for you I would have given them to you. Don't be so dumb, okay Ronnie you made your point I'll see you later when he left he gave her a kiss on the lips wishing it were in the mouth she couldn't help but to feel disappointed and hurt tears began to run down her face. He couldn't spend Valentines Day together she wanted to spend this special occasion with him and he's s spending it with his wife.

Cheryl knew she was acting selfish about this, she knew he's a married man and she would have to accept this or forget about it. The phone rang but it was Lynn calling to find out if she went out with Ronnie or not. Why the sad voice she asked, I'm upset she said. About what? Its Valentines Day you should be happy well I'm not Ronnie just left and had roses for his wife. Well what do you expect? The man's married she said he didn't have to let me see them and he had a nerve to say those are not for you did he get you anything? Yes He brought me some sunflowers. That's all she said you know if you're involved with a married man he's going to treat his wife better than a piece of ass on the side. I hate to hurt your feelings my dear. When men meet other women they are looking for something to fuck it's just that simple. But we haven't had sex yet, but ya'll will. I don't believe Ronnie is just after my body he gave me a dozen of flowers. As a matter of fact he's going out tomorrow to buy a bottle of Elizabeth Taylor Passion perfume. Yeh you wait on it, she thought Lynn was just saying negative things about Ronnie because she didn't have anyone to spend time with her. That man don't want you girl wake up and smell the coffee why won't you she said. Lynn could be mistaken about Ronnie, mistaken he's married so how can Cheryl be mistaken about a married man. I would like to continue this conversation but Ronnie is picking up in a couple of hours. Well think about what I said and I'll talk to you tomorrow, okay and they hung up.

Ronnie arrived that evening with a mean look on his face. Cheryl then asked him what's wrong. The Redskins lost the football game. Oh that's nothing she said smiling so what are we going to do on our date? Nothing I lost $300.00 dollars on that fuckin game. Are you ready to go and get my perfume? Are you crazy here I am telling you I lost my money and you're talking about buying your whoring ass some perfume? You don't even deserve nothing when are you going to fuck me, Or do I have to wait another 2 months, cause if you think I'm going to keep taking you out and spending my fuckin money on you and you're not trying to give me some pussy suck my dick then you're crazier then I thought. I didn't say I wasn't going to have sex with you. And since you're feisty than I think we should do this another day. No we should wait for nothing. Look Ronnie she said I'm leaving he then grabbed her arm I'm getting out of your car, good idea get your cheap ass out of my car bitch. It was going on 4:00 in the morning and Cheryl was walking down the dark streets that time of the morning he didn't even make a u-turn to pick her back up. Nonetheless she couldn't believe he threw her out of his car like she was a slut.

When she got home which was almost six in the morning, mascara was running down her face, along with the tears she had cried. Just a few hours later the phone rang and it was Lynn wondering why she was calling so early especially if she knew she would been asleep that time of morning but then she remembered she had told her that she was going out with him, So he can buy her some perfume. That didn't happen. Which Cheryl knew Lynn wanted the details, hey girl what's up? I'm upset right now she said. About what? Ronnie threw me out of his car. For what? He's mad because he lost some money on a Redskins game and because I wouldn't have oral sex on him. In others words he want you to have oral sex on him? Yes, he got angry also cause we haven't had sex yet. That nasty bastard you didn't do it did you? Well I called because my brother's girlfriend Michelle is related to Ronnie, small world isn't it. How are they related Ronnie is Michelle's godfather and he is married. I know that he explained everything to me. Why won't you leave that man alone girl he's no good for you, you're nothing to him, deep down inside she knew Lynn was right, she couldn't keep this fling going on for long and even seeing him another day for that matter, but she didn't want to be alone which at this point the only thing she needed to be concentrating on is graduating from school which her graduation was in two weeks. She needed to be focus on what is more important at this time, she then started thinking crazy, she thought maybe if I have sex and oral sex with him I'll have him all to myself.

She knew if she did that he would be happy, then she needed to know what made her happy which at this time in her life she didn't have a happy one. I probably never will she thought. She then needed to talk to her best friend, which is Lynn, the only friend she had. Cheryl told her that she thought about having sex with him and having oral sex, "are you crazy" she said shouting, he might leave her. Cheryl said, if you really believe if you suck that man dick he's going to leave his wife for you than you're a bigger fool than I thought she said, but Lynn that will make him happy, don't be trying to please that cystic-fibrosis head mutherfucker he's married any damn way, you should be trying to please yourself, Cheryl knew Lynn was telling the truth, the thought never crossed her mind until she talked to Lynn more and more about the situation that Ronnie want to have oral sex with her because his wife doesn't give him that and maybe that's the reason for him cheating on his wife you know Lynn you could be right, I know I'm right, it's getting late and I'm hungry ,not being cautious of what time it is, Lynn and Cheryl stayed on the telephone for three hours discussing Ronnie, which was a waste of time, she then went down stairs to get something to eat , rubbing her stomach, but mama already put the dinner back into the refrigerator, she couldn't warm it up cause they didn't have a microwave oven so then she placed the plate into the oven. She sat down at the table and ate which she couldn't finish because her mind was on Ronnie the rest of the night.

She tried to study for the test she had to take in a couple of days, but she still couldn't get her mind off of him, Cheryl then laid down to get some sleep. The next day he decided to call me apologizing. I'm sorry about what happened the other day, he said I can't accept your apology, why not, because you put me out of your car that's why, I could have been raped which that happened to me before, we were supposed to go to Hecht's to get some perfume. I told you I lost my money but that was not a reason to put me out of your car, yeh I thought about something could have happen to you, well I'm sorry please accept my apology it won't happen again. Okay she accepts. I tell you what. Next week I'm going to buy you a gold watch since I did not get you the perfume, actually I wanted the perfume she said to herself, are you busy now? No not at the moment. I'm on my way, where are we going you'll see.

By the time Ronnie arrived Lynn and Cheryl was still chitchatting on the phone. He's here now so I have to go, hey Darnell he said as he walked on the porch smelling like cologne and his red- and white baseball cap and white t- shirt and blue jeans we walked out to the car and started kissing and kissing until we had to stop the car. So then she slide close to Ronnie and they started kissing and hugging maybe if she gave him what he wanted maybe he will spend more time with her, Ronnie if we are going to sit here all night in this car and smooch then I could be out with the ladies tonight. Okay I'll drop you off he said and you can go out with your friends. Ronnie I know you're mad about me wanting to go out. Go ahead you just want to fool around with another man, Ronnie you're not in the predicament to be angry, so she gets out of the car and run into the house as she got into the house he was still sitting there waiting she yells out at him to tell him I'm alright I guess he just want to sit there and be stubborn but I'm going out and I don't care if he's mad or not she thought. So she calls Lynn and sees what she's doing, hey girl what's up as she answers the phone. Nothing just got home Ronnie dropped me off a couple of minutes ago.

She then told Lynn he had a nerve to get upset because I told him I'm wanna go out with the ladies what the hell is his problem I don't know I'm tired of going out to eat or making out in his car let him stay mad, shit he's married any way. She knew he was mad but in her mind she didn't felt guilty about going out we'll be there in one hour. When Lynn arrived Cheryl couldn't make up her mind about what she wanted to wear, I have nothing to wear. Come on girl, we'll find something for your ass to wear, so they get to her house rambling through her closet. Miss Paula comes into Lynn's room, Cheryl can you fit in this dress it was a red-pleaded dress. This is nice she said smiling. How do I look? Very conservative they both said let's go when they got there Cheryl decided to take a picture for Ronnie she knew when she show it to him his eyes might pop right out of his head. It was almost time to leave and she was overjoyed about coming out but she was anxious to get back home so she could talk to him as she got into the house everybody is sitting there watching TV. Anybody called she asked nobody but that Ronnie mama said sounding sarcastic, oh good I was hoping to hear from him. What's going on between you and this man anyway her mama said? We just go out together well I hope you're getting ready for your graduation next week I know all about that ma.

The phone then rang and it was Ronnie hey Darnell he said. I know this is not you sounding all cheerful and not being mad the way you acted yesterday you made me think you didn't like the idea of me hanging out no I didn't that's just too bad too bad for what that you're married and I'm not you can't tell me what to do don't talk back to me. Look I have another call Cheryl can I call you back. Ronnie where are you talking to me in the basement. Where's your wife? Upstairs folding my clothes, have you lost your mind she don't know who I'm talking to it's possible she can pick up the other line this is my phone line. There's two phone lines in this house Ronnie before you hang up, what? I love you okay bye, all she could do is stare at the four walls he didn't even tell me he love me too. I guess he don't care about me like I care about him, she thought about it that was foolish of me to even tell him I love him. I'm sure he don't love me he's married for god's sake. Tomorrow when I see him I'll tell him that I love him.

As she was laying in her room her mama tells her about an apartment as she was giving her a hint about moving out on her own she knew it was time that she moved on her own. But then again she get this apartment Ronnie can visit her it was no use really she don't have a job to pay the rent anyway. Mama I don't have any money the landlord's name is Mr. Myers call him tomorrow to discuss the apartment it's only $40.00 for the security deposit. How can I get that? Ask that so-called man you been going out with. What if he don't have it? I will give a try. The next morning she called Mr. Myers to ask him about the apartment. He informed that she will need to have a section 8 certificate which she didn't have one and was not sure what he was talking about, the next morning she caught the bus to 1133 North Capital St. which was the section 8 office when she got there the receptionist told her that the list is closed until next year. So come back saying it in a hostile voice later that evening she told Ronnie about the apartment. That's nice he said. But I need $40.00 for the security deposit. You want me to give you some money but I can't get my dick suck. Are you crazy? I don't need it that bad. That's the only way you're going to get it. I can't believe you would say something like that out of your mouth. We've been knowing each other for four months and we haven't slept together yet. Let's find something else to discuss. Like what. I wanna talk about you being married, I'm married so what. Now let's go. That's a good idea let's not argue everything is going to be fine. Can you take me home? For what, because I'm tired and exhausted it's all right with me Ronnie opens the car door and they pulls off. Ronnie where are we going you've been driving for at least an hour. Didn't you ask me to take you home? Yes I did. But it don't take this long, he then pulls in front of the Red Roof Inn on New York Ave. near the bus barn this is not where I live. I know I need a few hours of sleep before I go to work tonight he said. I see right now you're dishonest, I need to really get home look, you can rest here and that's all I have to say. Give me the number to call a cab I don't have the number to a damn cab company.

When he went to the bathroom, Cheryl rushed out of the room to catch a cab. As she was running she broke the heel off her shoe so she stood there at the corner waiting for a taxi. Which never showed up. It was getting late she then went back to the hotel room she guess she got cold feet cause she knew Ronnie wanted to sleep with her, and if she don't he would probably get angry and do something to her like kill her for instance when she got there he was sitting on the end of the bed waiting for her. You ain't shit. Ronnie, I just went out to see if I could catch a cab. I told you I was taking you home, I'm not going to bother you. Won't you tell me you don't want to sleep with me? I do feel a little uncomfortable. Why? You married. When are you going to lay down I'll lay down when I feel like it. Cheryl went to the bathroom to wash her face, Ronnie was laying there sleep in the nude she gets in the bed wondering what he is going to do. She really wants him to touch her but another part of her is saying no. Once she did lay down to get some rest he jumps up yelling do you know what time it is. Its 2:30 in the morning he was really rushing to put his clothes on even though he didn't try anything with her. Come on My wife is going kill me, and I miss work. Why did you come here in the first place? Shut the fuck up and get your stupid ass up so I can drop you off. They leave the hotel and he drops her off at her front door.

As she was waving at him to tell him goodnight he pulls off, instead of going in the house she sat on the front porch until 6:00 in the morning wishing that he had touch her. She needed it and wanted it had been a long time since she been touch. Cheryl felt herself getting sleepy she went upstairs to put on her flannel flowery nightgown. The next day she got up to wash clothes for her and Brian. She couldn't concentrate much on washing because she kept finding herself thinking about him, wishing he would have touch her that night she knew he wanted to. Because that's all he talks about. Or maybe he had something on his mind since she can't stop thinking about him she pages him the phone rings back and it was him. Hi Ronnie I just wanted to see what's on your agenda for today? Nothing really. Cheryl didn't know why she was being so nice to him considering the way he talked to her the other day. You wanna go see a baseball game today, sure she said. I'll pick you up around 3:30 this afternoon. Okay I'll be ready. Hangin up the telephone sounding overwhelmed about the baseball game knowing that she really don't know anything about sports but she would go anyway.

He finally shows up after 6: 00 in the evening what took you so long I had things to do with my wife is that okay. What time did the game start? It started at 4:00. Ronnie don't you think it's a little late to go? Yes I guess so, but we catch a movie. What's playing she asked we'll go somewhere else. Where? I'll surprise you. Ronnie what are you up to something? No, glancing over at her with a spurt on his face, I'm serious Ronnie thinking to herself that she really wanted to go the hotel. If she tells Ronnie is that where we'll be going he'll probably think very low of her. But then this is what both of them wanted. I knew this was the place you were taking me too. Why? Red Roof Inn it's a nice hotel I like the service they have, he gets the key from the receptionist as she was flirting with him. After he got the key she was right behind him knowing she wanted this to happen are you married she said being out of line. That's none of your business Ronnie said, are you okay Cheryl? No not really what's the matter she was flirting with you right in my face. You're not jealous are you? No I'm not deep down inside she shouldn't be mad he belongs to someone else. Let me make you feel better he begin to kiss her on the lips and then started to rub up and down her back and then they started kissing and kissing until things begin to get out of hand he tried to put his hands inside her vagina but then she quenched when she thought about being raped and that's how one of those dirty men done when they touched her down there, but she tried to relax, he stared into the ceiling and so was she at that time she thought they both would regret what could have happen.

She really didn't fell good about it, knowing he's married and then she wasn't comfortable attempting to have sex with him. Considering she was raped not to long ago, but she was trying to put it behind her. Ronnie do you feel guilty? No. Well I do for what? You're married. Here we go with this shit again. Do you feel guilty? Yes I do. Can I ask you question? Yeh what, I like oral sex he said I'm not into kinky sex. Are you ready to go? Yes I have to get ready for graduation in few days. Why can't we lay in each other's arms, cause I need to go Ronnie, you ain't going nowhere until you suck my dick. I'm not doing it. Yes you are, he then dragged her by her hair dragging her across the hotel floor, until he jabbed his penis into her mouth. Now get your ass up so I drop your ass off. They get into the car and he drops her off in the middle of nowhere. Ronnie, I don't know what your problem is but I'm not getting out of this car. Get the fuck out. Here's your funky ass panties as she got out of his car she slammed the car door, he jumps out and punch her in the face, it took her two hours to get home, and her mamma was worried. I don't know what's going on with you and that nigger you been going out with, but you need to stay your ass home.

He later called her that evening she really didn't want to talk to him, but she wanted to hear what he had to say, you're mad at me ain't you? Yes I am. I told you my wife don't like oral sex, I told you I don't like oral sex. Look I can get pussy from my wife, I don't need pussy from you, so you're telling me you just wanted to have oral sex with me? Exactly, that's all I need to hear. Can I see you? No, for what? You really hurt me. I'm sure you got home safely. I need to give you something. Like what? The $40.00 you asked me for. When he pulled up in front of the house, he noticed she was upset with him it's over he said, which she was glad he said that. Stop shredding those baby-tears, my wife found out about us, how? She saw the hotel receipt and you don't like sucking dick. And I need someone who likes that. And then he slid the $40.00 in her hand, she knew the way he drove off they really were through and she was relieved about his decision and hers.

Chapter 3

Thin Air

After graduation Cheryl was excited about how she could get a job and hopefully go to college and then get her own apartment, but then she decided to dance in the nightclubs to earn extra money to be able to pay for her apartment. Which she did that, but she knew it was risky to dance in the nightclubs, she heard that a lot of young women was getting killed in those places. The next day it was a nice and sunny day. So she decided to go job hunting, since she didn't know exactly where she was going she just rode around on the bus and put in job applications everywhere. She was going no one was excepting applications so she just kept riding until somebody was hiring, as she was riding the bus, she saw a sign where there was positions available for housekeeping, she got off the bus to apply for the job, She really did not want to do housekeeping but she had no other choice since her mama was giving her hints about working.

She had already applied for welfare so she could support her son since Darnell just gave up on their child, when she went inside not paying any attention to the advertisement that was on the glass window announcing sign read MUST HAVE A POLICE CLEARANCE BEFORE APPLYING FOR THE POSITION. Oh well she said I guess I'll comeback another day when I get it. So then she thought about dancing since she was good at it but she was shy about dancing in front of a room full of men, as she left the building she thought this was a drag, all this riding and walking form block to block just to find a job but she needed one. It was time she takes some responsibility for her and her son, and stop depending on her parents for everything. Or expecting someone else to stand ground when it was her who had to take charge.

When she got home and rest these tired feet of hers. That's been bothering all day long she felt really exhausted her hair was flying all over her head she was dripping with sweat all down her face smelling like a wet dog. When she got home she couldn't wait to take a shower which she needed so bad, she didn't know that job hunting could be so complicated but this is something she has to do, considering she had a child to take care of .the next day she didn't feel much like that get up and going, so she waited until next Monday she just hope that they haven't fill the positions for her sake. She hopes not. Then Monday came she got up around 7:00 that morning to the Municipal Center so that she can get my police clearance for the housekeeping job, the place was crowded and everyone had to get a number and be seated then they called her

Name to get fingerprinted she had to sit down to wait for her police record which was clear and no prior arrests. Well she was happy about that she couldn't wait until she got out of that place people were bunched up against one another. Now she thinking to herself what's going to happen with the housekeeping job, she took a chance to apply for it if I don't get it at least it was a try. Because now she waited a whole week she went through the building that was nicely kept. The receptionist asked her, may I help you? As she gave her police clearance you can hold on to that just sign your name on the clipboard. Here's an application have a seat and fill it out, the application was confusing to fill out because this was the first job she have ever applied for.

When she finished the application she was called in for an interview there was so many questions she didn't know how to really answer them, so she answered then the best to her ability. Due to her incapability when the man handed her the blue smock she was wondering what this is for. Not knowing she was hired right on the spot. She started the same day. When Cheryl left she went to the night spot where she was suppose to dance. Which she was quite nervous the first couple of days. It was very tiring especially going to school even after graduation, to get brushed up on some work that she didn't master awhile she was there. And going to general maintenance and then the nightclub she was beginning to get frustrated at that point. But she knew she couldn't keep up with the fast lane when it came to dancing in the nightclub, and especially if her mama found out. She would she explain that she was shaking my ass in front of a bunch of crazy men and most of them were married or did not have anything else to do. She thought about quitting. After my first day she was so overjoyed that she had a job now she treated herself to lunch now she have a job she can spend some extra money.

She wasn't sure where she wanted to eat, so she went to McDonald's and had a Big Mac with French fries and a large orange soda. She just sitting there eating not realizing how she going to get home since she spent her bus fare on lunch. Now she's getting paranoid. When she finished her meal she looked in her purse to see if she had any more money, which she found a dollar. Way down in her pocketbook, and then strutted out of McDonald's with her see through white-skirt on. Asking people for directions she asked one guy how I get to the subway Station, he did not know. Now she's getting frustrated she was asking everyone for directions. She was so miserable she sat down on a bench. These two guys walked over to her. At that time she got a little frightened. She then heard one of them say you look good in your skirt and the other said she looked trifling. She knew they were talking about her. But she was too tired to pay them any attention. I'll just get home the best way I know how she thought, after going through the hassles with the job. She went straight home to tell her mama the good news. Mama Mama! Guess what?

I found a job at General Maintenance Cleaning Company I'll be cleaning the office building down town. That's good news her mamma said. I start

Monday here's my smock this is what I have to wear. I don't know where I will be cleaning at as of yet but I'll find out the day I go in. good. Now you can give me some rent money, I haven't even started yet and you're asking me for money. Don't get smart witch. You need to take your ass down there to sign up for Public Assistance. The next day Cheryl and her mama went to the Department of Social Services they got there waiting in the line for nearly an hour and a half. All for nothing, to be told she was too young to apply and to come back in a year when she turns 18 which she was turning 18 in 3 months.

The social worker there was very hostile, all she kept saying was come back in a year, she can get the check for mama said. No mama the worker so rudely said, all you mean ass bitch mama said. At least Cheryl had a job to go to on Monday. It was kind of hectic trying to go to school which she have already graduated, but you never seem to finish school. And then going to work in the evenings and dancing in the nightclubs which she will stop soon. Ever since I had been dancing in the hole in the wall she has been feeling shameful. Especially since she has not told her mama she was a nighttime stripper. The next day she went to school and go to work and the nightclub, but that's something she have to get used doing, when she left school that afternoon she was so excited and a little tense about going to work, as she was getting off the bus catching another bus to work she was sort of feeling scared because it was getting dark so she walked pass a construction site, where a lot of guys were working she heard whistling on the street, hey! Come here sexy as they were trying to get her attention, she felt bashful sort of, but she enjoyed the attention. She felt like a movie star. It was one guy trying to get her attention. Hey don't pay knuckleheads no mind. Why? Cause I like you can I get some digits, he said. Okay here's my number call me sometime she said smiling here I go again she thought, what's your name? Its David it means the greatest of all time he said laughing, well give me a call. By the way where are you going he said, to work? Today is my first day where do you work; at the Willard Hotel it's just a few blocks away. If I didn't have to stay here tonight and work, I'll be glad to take you he said. No that's all right I can make it from here. How came you called your co-workers knuckleheads? Cause they are, they're always trying to pick up on women. What about you? You came up to approach me. Yeh that's because I'm a gentleman. Okay, I see you must have had a bad experience. Somewhat. I figure that. I can tell by looking at you. I better get going. Being on time on the first day is the best impression. I can dig it, he said. Call me she said.

As she got in the building there was lot of supervisors passing out duty sheets. When they gave her the duty sheet she was advised to clean the restrooms and then vacuum. She couldn't understand it for only $4.25 an hour, all this work she would have better off cleaning the streets. Well it's better than nothing at all. By the end of the day she was so exhausted, it was time to punch out. Since she was so tired she had no energy to go to the club. She couldn't wait to get away from those chemicals that were so strong. It was going on 11:30 at night, so she walked 5 blocks to the bus stop. Cheryl couldn't believe nobody was out there it was like being in the Boone docks. She wishes she had David's number, but he didn't give to her. She would tell him to pick me up.

The next day she went in to work, she felt so tired but she knew she had to do the job as she was sitting down at one of the desks that were in the middle of the suites, the elevator was coming up on the floor where she was assigned coming out of the elevator was her assigned supervisor, his name was Clark. Hi, I'm taking a break; I'll get back to work. I'm sorry she said in a timid voice. It's okay. He said. Are you sure? Yes I'm sure so you like this kind of work, huh. It's all right it's good to have some extra money in my pocket. I have a little boy I have to take care of. Is that right, can I ask you something to you without you thinking I'm being fresh He said. Sure. May I kiss you? What? Are you crazy she shouted call me bluff, I think you better go downstairs. He began grabbing her by the arm and slid his tongue in her mouth. Stop please stop. You are my supervisor what are you doing?

Cheryl couldn't do anything so she went to the bathroom to wash her face. She knew he had followed her in there. Clark I think you should do your job, Instead of chasing me around this hotel. But I want you, is there something wrong with that? Yes it is. What? You're my supervisor. How would that look if we start dating each other? You're so sexy. I don't care what you say this isn't right. If someone find you up here trying to come on to me. We're in deep trouble; I can't afford to loose my job. What makes you think I'll risk our jobs for a few hours of passion? It won't be any passion. If you want this job it will be some passion. You need to feed your kid, than I suggest you better follow through with the plans. When he caught the elevator downstairs she flopped down in the chair feeling nervous knowing if she didn't do what he said she would be fired. When she went downstairs to punch out, she couldn't even look him in the eyes. She was so embarrassed about what had happened. She couldn't wait til she got out of there, and go home as soon she go the club for a few hours, and go home to do some homework. Or maybe she would do it on the bus. After the club she was so tired when she got home putting her purse and plastic bag full of junk and realized that David left 4 messages on her answering machine.

Cheryl felt so happy to hear that he called. So she called him back. Hello, who is this? I may ask. Acting as though she didn't know which she did when she heard the voice on the voice mail. This is Dave. Hi David. You don't remember me oh yes I do. How are doing. I thought I had the wrong digits, at first he implied. No you called the right number. Trying to come out to tonight? I don't know it's kinda late and I have to go school in the morning just for a couple of hours. Since she just have to turn in this paper she'll just drop it off before she have to go to work. I can scoop you up right quick. David where are from? You don't sound like you're from Washington D .C. I'm from Philadelphia and where are you from? I'm from Washington D. C. I wanna know where are you taking me to this time of night? For a joy ride is there something wrong with that. In a way yes. Are you coming or not? Yes just for a little while.

Cheryl couldn't believe her eyes he had the same blue-Volvo exactly like Ronnie's. She just had to feel his soft light-skinned complexion. His face felt so soft and then they pulled up in front of a brown-brick building with dull-sided windows. David is this where you live. No this is my sister's house. Don't you think you should have called first? She don't mind if we come here. Come for what? She knew when he didn't take me to his house; she knew he was hiding something. I been through this before but I 'm not going through this same nightmare again she thought to herself. I think we should leave before your sister wakes up. Look, I'm being straight up with you I want sex. We barely know each other. Come on baby, my dick is solid hard. She knew she wanted it as much as he did. It has been a long time since she had sex and it's not like they have to see each other again. But then if the sex is good maybe, they can do this again. I don't feel comfortable having sex in your sister's house. She's not going to bother us. David I'm not sleeping with you. Is that the reason you brought me up here? I want some pussy. He then pushed her against his sister's diner table with her dress pulled up and he rammed his penis into her vagina very forcefully. Stop she said loudly but his sister would not come out. Shut up Bitch. I'm not hurting you. Give me that pussy you know you want it. You didn't even kiss me or anything I'm particular about kissing anyone. So that's how you caress a woman. By forcing yourself on them. Who wants to kiss your chap lips? Your vagina feels like you can put a baseball inside. Your toes look like fingers. I guess all you wanted was sex. Bingo, just take me home. Gladly he said. When he drove her home, she felt so embarrassed se then thought it was her fault for leaving with him. She didn't even know him. He seemed like such a gentleman at least that's what he told her when she met him. The next day she went to work but she really didn't feel like going.

Since Clark was hounding her like a dog. She then wanted to report him to the Immediate Supervisor for sexual harassment. But then again she needed her job. So she could support her son. When she left so she could go to the club and dance. David was sitting in his car waiting for her After what happen last night she didn't think he wanted to see her anymore or more the less she wanted to see him. Again. What are you doing here? She asked in a calm but simple voice. I thought you might want a ride home. I can make it from here. Anyway I have something else to do. What? Go dance in that nightclub. How did you know about that? You remember the day you met me. One of the guys recognized you in that whore's convention. That's what I call it. Are you coming or not, she then gets in the car. Well it's easy to say this but I'm going back to Philadelphia. I'm not going to miss you. You raped me. I did not rape you. I told you to stop and you kept being persistent on having sex with me instead of waiting until I was ready. And then you came down here to tell me that you're going back to Philadelphia? The whole time they were riding she said nothing in regards to his smart comment. In the back of her mind she knew he was married.

Cheryl guesses that's why he brought her to his sister's house. As she got out of the car she just slammed his car door and he drove off. She didn't even attempt to look back to see his reaction. She just wanted to get as far away from him as possible, but something inside of her kept saying, I have to see him before I go back to Philadelphia. Tomorrow I'll catch the bus over to his sister's house. By the time she arrived David's car was parked outside. His sister answered the front door in such an angry voice, is David here yes he is he's in the restroom. Hey, as he came out. So full of excitement, hunting me down, huh, with sweat balls all over his forehead. No I just took my chances of coming over here. I don't have time to discus this I have to run to the store. She now was waiting for three hours for him to return. But she just sat there talking to his sister. Honey I don't mean to get in your business but my brother is not being truthful with you. Why would you say that? Well he's married and has three boys; his wife has been calling me for two days looking for him. He don't live here? He just came to visit me and my husband. And he's going back to Philly on Friday. It's something else you need to know about David, he's a liar. I met him on a construction site. He just went to one of those Union jobs since he was visiting for a month; he has a really good job in Philly. This guy has been calling here from Philly too. Why has his wife been calling if she knew he was visiting? That's because he supposed to go back on last week. Why has the guy been calling him? Is that a friend of his? Trying to get information. It was no use since she found out he's married. This might burst your bubble David sister said, the guy's voice was a little soft I think the guy is gay. And him and David's been fooling around. When he called he was sounding upset, asking me if David is coming back. And also David had stolen some merchandise from him. That's why my brother went to the bathroom for so long. You're telling me he's on drugs. Exactly, and I told David he needs to go home, before he gets his self hurt out here in D. C. So I don't know what he told you but my brother needs to be honest with these women and stop lying about his situation. You're not the only woman who came here looking for David. But he's leaving tomorrow, which is Friday. I'm sorry I don't even know your name, it's Carol. Well Carol do you know when David is coming back? I really couldn't tell you sweetie. I had no idea that he was married you sound just like the other girl that came here a week ago. Where is she? She told David she ain't taking his bullshit. And she left she actually tried to break his windows out of his car. Until he knocked her ass on the ground, he hits women. He hits his wife. I don't know why Karen stays with him all these years. But she loves him so much and then they have three boys, so I guess that's why she's there. He better bet his lucky stars I don't talk to Karen on a regular basis and tell her his ass is cheating on her left and right. But as stupid as she is she wouldn't believe it anyway. Does his wife know he's cheating on her with a man? Probably do. Karen don't care. She loves David's funky ass underwear. He comes down here every year and pick up a woman just so he can get in there underwear. I overheard when he brought you over here and forced his self on you. But I didn't want to get involved. He treats his wife the same way. He met that other girl at that same construction site. He just seems to be such a gentleman at first. Why would you want to see him again if he forced you into sex, I don't know, I guess I wanted it as well but he didn't give me a chance. Well Carol, I guess I better be going. What's your name? It's Cheryl. Ok it was nice talking to you Cheryl.

As she got to the bottom of the steps she saw David snorting cocaine from a dollar bill. Where are you going he asked? Home. She couldn't even look back at him. She just kept walking. She knew if she did she would have been facing a dramatic situation.

Chapter 4

No Love Lost

It was May 1988, there was a terrible shooting, and it was the wrong time for Cheryl and her friend Carla to be walking, that time of the night just to get a soda from the corner store. But they both were thirsty by the time they came out of the store the police and the ambulance was surrounding the store. At that time the paramedics were lifting a body up off the ground, it was a crazy night in S. E. D. C. Sirens was going off It wasn't no surprise someone was always getting shot or killed in that area. It probably was another drug-related killing Cheryl assumed it was because Carla and her saw the guy as they were picking him from the ground. People were crowded in the middle of the streets. What Cheryl overheard was the guy was 16 years old and was shot 11 multiple times in the head. The mother was terribly upset jumping and down near the body. Sometimes she wish that this kind of mischief never existed' but if you're out there selling drugs; this is the situation you will be facing.

When the uproar was over Carla and Cheryl was terrified that something could happen to them both. Cheryl couldn't stop shaking. There were people everywhere standing and watching the paramedics place the guy in the ambulance. Others were hanging out of their windows. Some were yelling, screaming over the lost. Cheryl stood there in shock and so was Carla. Because she never saw nobody killed or more the less shot. She couldn't believe all this confusion went on. When Cheryl turned around it was a guy standing by a tree, he somewhat look suspicious. Did you see what happen cutie? Yes I did It was horrible Cheryl said still in shock. That's a shame he said. Can I get you name? It's Cheryl and I must be going. And it's getting late I don't have time to chitchat. Come on girl, he might be the murderer Carla said. No I don't think so, He's cute Carla. He favors Larry Fishborne. Go on and be a fool, you just got out of some bullshit. It don't mean this will be a relationship said Cheryl.

So they stood there for a couple of minutes and exchanged phone numbers at least he gave her his home phone number. Come on Cheryl, I don't have time to stand here and watch you talk to some man. And by the way what's your name? Anthony. All right Anthony give me a call. That's his name yeh? Look at you grinning, It's strange but unique Carla said. I know it's rare you hear somebody would have a name like that. As they all walked off, Cheryl and Carla was still shaken up over the murder, and really scared when they walked through the alley, which they had to take another route. Anthony couldn't wait to call Cheryl, she was only in the house for an hour and the phone rang. They were on the phone for four and a half hours. The conversation they were having got to be boring. He was turning her off at some of the jive he was saying. Anthony and Cheryl didn't have anything in common. He's trying to put on this suave attitude. This was hardly working in her vocabulary she don't think she, want to date him he really didn't have a job, all he did was pump gas at the gasoline station. And she was sure he didn't even have enough money to take her on a date, let alone car. Which she didn't have one either. She guesses she shouldn't put him down and she was working at general maintenance, and working in the nightclubs stripping for a bunch of nasty greasy men. She couldn't judge him, cause everybody needs love. The way Anthony was talking she thought it's better for them to remain friends.

When she decided to call him she told him it's best for us to be friends but he insisted on pursing a relationship with her. Telling her how he would love to spoil her with luxury items. Which all of this sounded good, the first thing came to her mind was did he have a job? She then asked him all of these things you're supposed to be buying me, are you employed? Then she thought I wasn't looking for someone to buy me things. I was looking for somebody to respect me, which so far I wasn't getting. The question you asked me no I didn't have a job, but I goes to the gas station and pump gas for now. That's all? I can't believe you don't have a job, and telling me how much you're going to spend on me.

Unless you're slinging drugs. No my father will help me out. Do you stay with your father? Yeh I do. Can you meet me at Fletcher Johnson tomorrow? For what? I wanna see you.

When they hung up she didn't see that being possible since she had a full schedule. Cheryl wanted to go the club and then next day she was quitting cause she knew sooner or later somebody will recognize her in there. She missed school the next day just so she could meet Anthony at the school. When they talked she told him give her a couple of hours to get dressed. He was really desperate, he must have been waiting every since they hung up the phone. How long have you been standing down here? For a while, waiting for my new queen? Is this your way of getting in my heart? You can say that, because telling me you're going to buy me expensive gifts is not going to work? Especially, when you don't have a job to begin with. I have a job but it's something small. I told you I pump gas. You don't get a paycheck for it now do you? No people just give me money for putting the gas pump in their car. I'm ashamed a little for doing that. You should never be ashamed of your accomplishments, tell me something how you can afford to take care of me if that's your only source of income? Unless you doing something else. I'm selling drugs if that's what you are thinking. I don't go out with guys just to receive material things from them. It's how a man treats me and their personality. Anthony are we going to stand here and talk or what?

Rubbing his hands through his curly hair, Pants barely on his ass. She felt disappointed on the way he was dressed but she guess that was his style. They decided to take a walk to his house. Cheryl knew he was up to no good if they were going to his house, but she paid that no attention cause she has to be strong about her flesh. Which was so weak especially pertaining to sex. The building in which he lived smelled of old fertilizer and old urination. Closing her nose as she walked up those heap of steps. She was now getting tired, what floor you live on? She asked out of breath. On the 5th floor Right here. About time. When we get there she was gonna fall out. They were both laughing.

When they went inside, there was an old man sitting in a chair. Oh this is my father Mr. Davis. Hello she said. Bye, she was ready to leave. Anthony, your father is rude. I think I better leave. No don't go. He's always acting so mean. But he's not very friendly when people come in his home. Wanna come back? For what she said. As though she don't know what he wanted, which she did. No, I'm not coming in your bedroom. She knew the minute she stepped in Anthony's room he would try to come on to her, in other words he did. She resisted at first. But then she couldn't when they started kissing and hugging. As bad as she needed somebody to hold her, she would give in, and that's exactly what she did. They couldn't stop kissing, after it was all over with. He did some extraordinary things to she that no man she had ever been with did.

It was wild lovemaking even oral on his part. She had never had that done to her; it was a thing she could get use to. Anthony can I ask you something Cheryl said. yeh sweetheart. Here we go with the sweet and kind attitude, she thought to herself, Later on he'll be acting just like a jackass. Have you did this to any other girl's you been with? No you were the first. Come on I'm serious. I love you Cheryl. We barely even know each other. We can get to know each other if you let me know you better he said. With a grin on his face, let's take a shower together he said and they did. They started having sex in the shower and he rubs her brown soft thighs and then took his tongue and kissed all inside her womanhood just the way she liked it. And then slid his penis inside her womanhood she couldn't take it anymore it was getting intense with pleasure. Cheryl loved every minute of it.

They then got out of the shower. He seemed to be excited about what he was doing to her. She noticed his male-ego overwhelming him. She knew she had to keep her eyes open on this one as well. She don't want to get her hopes up on him. The only thing Cheryl was attracted to was his lovemaking guess that's what they will have in common. She noticed pictures of girls on his wall are these your girlfriends, ex-girlfriends? He said in a hurry, they mean nothing to me. You're the best woman I have ever been with. She was trying to figure him out telling her he's going to spoil her then he loves her, and she's the best he's been with. Full of lies, she kept telling herself over and over again putting her clothes on so she could go to work and then to the club. Which she knew she was quitting the strip club soon. Considering it was taking a toll on her body, trying to get home to take care of her son. Which her time needs to be dedicated more with him. Deep down she knew he was lying. Anthony, that's flattering if you want us to be together. Just ask? Cheryl it's the truth he said, so are you going to be my lady? Yes she said. So you want some Chinese food I am getting hungry.

As they walked to the Store he couldn't stop holding her hand. What would you like? Some shrimp fried rice and one egg roll please; tell them to give you extra soy sauce. Anything for you baby. You're not getting anything to eat? No I'm too excited to eat. About what? About us baby, and this is just the beginning of our relationship. You can get anything you want from me. Anthony, I have somewhere I have to go tomorrow. So I'm going to have to hurry and eat this when we get back to your house, and plus I have to see my son and feed him it's getting late. So don't get carried away with me coming over to see you. Why not? I have to get up tomorrow to go downtown, so I can enroll in School I'm getting my certificate in computers. Where is this school? Stop asking me so many questions, I told you and that's all you need to know. Call me I gotta go Cheryl said. The next day she went to sign up for school, and the following week she started her classes at PTC Career Institute for Data Entry, at that time her mind wasn't focusing on Anthony or any man for that matter.

Cheryl was so busy with her homework and her classes and was excited about going. When she went to work she wanted the supervisor to change her hours so she can attend school in the morning since she had completed the other school for word processing, but then she was called to the office, saying she was fired for unknown reasons. She knew what this was all about, just because she wouldn't sleep with Clark. It had to be probable cause for terminating her. She just walked out feeling sad and depressed she then knew she was quitting the nightclub and now she had to go welfare so that she can support her son. Now she would have to concentrate on her studies instead of wandering about Anthony or anybody else. As soon as class let out Anthony was they're waiting for her at the bus stop. It was late she had to take evening classes since she lost her job. What are doing down here? I need $2.00 you come all the way down here for $2.00? Here. This is ridiculous she said in an angry voice. Here you are bragging about what you are going to do for me. So what? Damn it. Anthony do me a favor Go Home! I can handle myself. Girl it's dark out here. I can't let you go home by yourself. Who ask you to bring your ass down here In the first place? I had to get $2.00 from you. So you really didn't come down here to make sure I get home safely? Yeh that too. That's just crazy. Your father can't loan you any money? Don't act stingy Cheryl some money is on the way to me real soon. And when I get it I'll share some with you. Good for you Anthony. You're making me mad with your got-so-much attitude. Just stay the hell away from me.

Cheryl felt kind of bad the way she talked to Anthony but she wasn't about to accept any lies he was telling her. It don't matter anyway he's not her type of man. By the time she got home she could not sleep, it was going on 3:00 in the morning, she guess a lot had to do with her was getting tired of dancing, so tomorrow I 'm quitting she thought. She really was doing it cause she thought by now she would be living in her own apartment. Which she should be by now, She didn't make much money cause she was too shy most of the time. By the time Cheryl got up Anthony was ringing her telephone off the hook. Begging for her to talk to him. I don't want to hear nothing from you Anthony. Meet me at the bottom of the hill across the street from Fletcher Johnson School Cheryl. Are you breaking up with me? You can say that. But why? You're asking me for money, and then you're a liar. I can't take any of this. In her mind, she wanted to leave him because he didn't have a car, which she didn't either. As she tripped up on the front porch mat trying to get out of the front door, mad as she was she didn't care much about falling. I wanted to call it quits. Cheryl give me a chance. No I can't. Just hand over my pictures I gave you, and find somebody else to lie to.

When she got back her mama asked her who's the secretive man she was sneaking around with was? After being on a warpath, He's a friend I just got rid of Ma. I'm not going to school today. Why not? I don't feel good I'm going to my room to get some rest. By the end of the day she was still feeling woozy, the only thing she can think of was she could be pregnant, and she knew having another child right now wouldn't be a good choice. She was not in a good predicament to become pregnant, so she went to Greater Southeast Hospital to get tests, she sat there waiting for her to be seen when they decided to call her name she got really nervous about what the results will be. The nurse calls her to sit in the room and then she brought the lab work in. Cheryl your blood test shows you're positive, you're pregnant. Cheryl rushed out of those revolving doors; all she could do was stand near the closest bridge.

Everything was closing in on her. She had lost her first and only job, since she quit the nightclub, and now she's pregnant with her second child. What's next? Cheryl was feeling suicidal and depressed, Mama is going to kill me she thought, and there was no sense of me hiding it. Such as she did with the first pregnancy, so she went home to tell her right away. Before she finds out from one of her noisy sisters. Ma, I have something to tell you Cheryl said. What is it? Spill it out kid. The way she responded Cheryl knew she would be upset, I'm pregnant again. I should have known that shit anyway. Are you angry? Should I be, tell that punk you fooling around with I am. But I don't know he's going to take it ma, the way I acted towards him last week he might hang the phone up on me. Cheryl wanted to call Anthony and tell him, I'll just wait until I get to school tonight she thought.

As much as he's been chasing her around he might be excited about the news. It's no sense in waiting she better tell him before she gets too far in her pregnancy. As she was standing at the phone booth that was right behind her heel. He said answering the phone in a raspy voice; my voice sounded a little bitter when he answered what's up? He said glad to hear from you. You gonna take me back? No, I just call to tell you something, I'm pregnant. What? You crazy as shit my girl can't get pregnant, how can you get that way? How the hell you think I got this way? We had sex don't you remember. Yes I remember. You're telling me you have a girlfriend already, you don't want me? No I don't, I can't handle all of your boasting. I told you in the beginning I'm not dating anyone for money. You don't have to impress me by telling me a bunch of lies Cheryl said. Okay you had your words goodbye and hung up. She then threw her pocketbook onto the ground she really couldn't get mad at him. She ended this fling in which it was called. Cheryl was so angry she couldn't find the words she wanted to say. The next day she went to school her instructor and classmates surprise her with a baby shower, she felt so excited about the gifts she received, the argument she had with Anthony didn't even bother her.

After he hangs up the phone on her, she was finished with him for good. Cheryl was getting at the end of her pregnancy and she was more on focusing on education and having her child, which tomorrow she will find out what the baby is. As big as her belly was she quit the club just in time. As months were prolonging Anthony started coming over more frequent. Which she felt sick whenever he showed his lying face? She would ask him what did he want every time he came over. I want you baby is what he would say, but she was no where near interested in him, after he told her he was with someone else. You have a girlfriend not anymore? Well, Anthony I'm now eight and a half months pregnant I don't need you. Can I have some? Some what? Pussy. I don't think so; sounding harshly telling him meant nothing. Cheryl didn't know why she gave in to him at that time she really felt lonely, about sleeping with him, She never loved him she guess it was infatuation.

All she wanted to do was leave, it was bad enough she slept with him in her parent's house after she got what she wanted she told him to leave. I wanna rub your stomach he said, you haven't been rubbing it. Why now?

A couple of hours later that morning Cheryl went into labor the next thing she knew water was gushing from her "mama mama' she ran downstairs to her bedroom here's a towel her mama gently placed the towel in her pants, what's going to happen she kept repeating in her mind, as she kept pulling up the baggie sweat pants she was wearing, then water started gushing once again she was scared she didn't know what to do. This is all Anthony's fault. Cheryl can't believe it's time for her to deliver it's too early she thought, I'm only 8 months as time went by she started to get worried. Ma when is the ambulance coming? Calm down they'll be here shortly. Just a few minutes later a siren was going off. Well, it's about time they showed up, cause she didn't want to loose her baby. As she took a deep breath afraid of what may happen when the paramedics gently grabbed her by the armpit and sat her down in the wheelchair. Cheryl started to bleed from her urine.

Tears begin running from her eyes, hurry she yelled at the paramedics. Are you all right no I'm bleeding? Just hold on. Cheryl couldn't wait until she got to the hospital she was immediately taken to the triage to be examined. Lets induce her labor, one nurse demanded. As the hospital staff was crowding her, Cheryl's throat began to get dry, but she couldn't have any thing to drink, which was the rules. The contractions were getting closer and closer, lying down suffering all over again with labor pains kinda had her wondering why am I going through this all over again. I barely can take care of Brian and then I gets pregnant she thought. As the pains became stronger it was time for her to be rolled into the delivery room. She breathed a sigh of relief as she lied there and received the hypodermic needle to relieve this intensifying pain. The intern asked was she ready to push, but when she did she started to cry, thinking how and would I be able to take care of another child. A couple hours later Cheryl gave birth to a 9 pound 9 ounces baby girl,

She was really tired and excited at the same time. The nurse brought the baby over to Cheryl, she was cold and wet she couldn't stop staring into her eyes she was so beautiful and cuddly. Mama would you like to hold her Cheryl asked yes as she reached for her first granddaughter who do you thing she looks like mama Cheryl asked. She looks like Anthony, and speaking of the devil I need to call him and tell him he has a baby girl Cheryl said. Two days Cheryl was lying in the hospital waiting to go home with her beautiful daughter, two days passed and today she was going home. When her mama picked her and Tylanya up there was a long wait for the taxicab. Cheryl was getting frustrated when they arrived home she was very tired and miserable. A week went passed and Anthony has not showed up yet, I really didn't care I guess he didn't care whether he has a daughter or not Cheryl thought.

Chapter 5

Promises

After three months, Anthony showed up to see their daughter, Cheryl couldn't believe he had a nerve to show up after all this time, but she let him see her, it wasn't any use of being selfish about it. The next couple weeks later Cheryl decided to get in with a modeling agency, since she wanted to be a model since she was ten years old. There they were all dressed up in our glamorous dresses Cheryl and her friend Becky, she only knew her for one year but they got along as thought they have been knowing each other for years. They were waiting for their interviews with a guy to take their pictures for a modeling agency, but something was somewhat strange about the whole ordeal it wasn't an agency, they had to meet him in a barber shop located on Minnesota Ave. N. E. There was no fee to be paid for this so- called agency; this was too good to be true anxious as Cheryl was to become a fashion model she really hope this thing goes well. Since nothing else was going perfect all she could think about was walking down a runway with a lot of people watching her and clapping their hands waving and laughing, smiling, taking her pictures, all that glamour and success. She couldn't wait til she showed off her fusia ruffled laced dress with her back out and breast puffed up. Becky and Cheryl were anxious to meet this guy, strutting down the streets smiling at everyone that passed them. "Becky do you think we are being tricked into something? Cheryl asked. No girl come on, it's just a try if we don't make it so what. Cheryl said what you mean if we don't make it? I want to make I always wanted to be a model this is a one and a lifetime chance for us. I'm going to be worried if we don't make it. I worry that it's to good to be true.

When they got there he as asked them to have a seat, while he set a projector just a few minutes he said, don't worry it's okay I been doing this for years. He then came out of this room with a dingy colored curtain looking like they haven't been washed in a while. It's one-thing ladies I need for both of you to undress for me said. For what Cheryl jumped from her chair. It's not like that; oh by the way my name is Greg. Can I get you ladies name? I'm Cheryl and I'm Becky. Please to meet both of you. I thought your name is Mr. Perfect Cut? No that's just my Barbershop name if you go outside it's on the top of the building. Get undress. Are you out of your cock-pickin mind Cheryl knew it was something fishy about this whole modeling business, this procedures not in my book she said angrily I'm not taking off a single shred of clothing. Well since your girlfriend ain't interested how about you Becky? Why do we have to take off our clothes? No I don't mean that ya'll get naked baby. Well what do you mean? I said I have some bikinis you two can slip on, come on girl this might be our big break Becky said. No you go right ahead Cheryl just stood there with her arms folded she couldn't believe Becky fell for this scam, and she so much wanted for this to be real. Becky do you see those photographs on the wall of all those exotic women? So what. That don't mean we going to be like that. How would you know, this guy is pulling our leg and we're too dumb to see it, but he can pull your leg cause I'm outta here said Cheryl this business is not legit. We might get raped or something we don't even know this man and getting raped is not what want to happen to me especially, or you. Girl we ain't going to get raped. What if we get killed nobody knows where we were going to in the first place. Well I told my mother where I was going she said, shaking her head. Did you tell yours? Not exactly, I told her we were going to a modeling agency. But see, Cheryl said, that's the point we're not at a modeling agency, it's a barbershop. What if he wants to have sex with us? I doubt it. How would you know? Why is he holding his business in a barbershop anyway? Think about it Becky you can do what you wanna do, I 'm leaving. Don't leave me here with this man. This man don't have a contract or anything Becky, don't be so knave. Do you like red roses? See Becky that's his contact, you better open your eyes or you keep them shut. What is this just so you can butter us up, so we can dazzle you with our bodies. No I'm a gentleman.

Soon as he gave them those red roses Cheryl's attitude change, she never got red roses from anybody not even her children's fathers but it still didn't change the way she felt about trying to get them to take off their clothing. When he finished showing off his camera and showcase of other models it was getting late and Cheryl had to get up early in the morning, but when Greg gave them those roses she felt really bad about how she talked to him. Can I give both of you ladies a ride? If you would accept it. Why not? It's late anyway. Cheryl couldn't believe what she saw when they got outside he had a gray-jaguar a Kawasaki motorcycle with his name on the license plate a ski-blue thunderbird Becky do you see what I see Cheryl ask, What are you talking about girl? Look at all those vehicles he has. Yeh I know maybe this modeling business is for' real. All of sudden you're changing your mind cause you saw his cars and why is that? Well Becky it could be some truth to this now that I see some profit from it. What profit the jewelry, cars, and he is sexy I'm going to tell him what you said. Don't do that smiling, and if you do he wouldn't be interested in someone like me anyway. Girl stop putting yourself down. Look at all the luxury he has and what do I have, nothing that compared to his stylish ass. It was the roses wasn't it? No it wasn't the roses after I saw the paperwork and those portfolios of those other girls, that's what made me change my mind. Girl you wild Becky said, Maybe her mind was playing tricks on her, Cheryl you need to stop thinking this way, she kinda felt something like a crush on Greg the roses did play a big part in it, she told herself over and over

I'm going to leave these men alone for a while, but she can't think all men is bad.

Becky and Cheryl had another appointment at 6:00, which was good because Cheryl just wanted to go back there and stare into his hazel-brown eyes. Hello ladies nice to see both of you again. Good to see you again Cheryl said with a smile on her face. Your attitude sure did change all of sudden Cheryl. Why would you say that? You smiling and blushing and everything. Maybe because I'm in a good mood Cheryl said. That's good to hear. I know why she' blushing Becky said, let me tell you Greg pulling him by the arm. Cheryl knew at the time what Becky was telling him it was like they were back in High School sending messages to a boy we liked. Cheryl can I see you for a minute he said smiling? Did you tell Becky? I was sexy uh? Cheryl's heart begins to pound when he asked her, Becky what did you say? Well she said with a sigh, you did say he was sexy. But you didn't have to tell him. I could have told him, okay I said it Greg. Why thank you I'm flattered to know that. Can I speak with you privately? Okay Cheryl said can you meet me down here tomorrow alone? What about Becky she said with her mouth hung open? Cheryl I wanted to tell your sexy too, stop pulling my leg you're just saying that because I told you, because if you wanted to tell me I was sexy you would have without hesitating. No seriously I need to see you, come here for a minute. What? I wanna kiss your soft tender looking lips. No Greg, I'll just meet with you tomorrow. He put his arms around Cheryl and started kissing her was like they were in a movie putting their tongues in each other's mouths, she so badly wanted this she just couldn't resist him. This shouldn't have happen Greg. You know we both wanted this so stop pretending. Okay, he said 7:00. Okay she said you got it. Come on Becky, we must go putting her pocketbook on her shoulder. What happen back there Becky asked? Nothing. Yes it did I'm not stupid she said. We just talked he wants me to come tomorrow at 7:00 in the evening. Bullshit I can't believe you two was back there just talking just to be communicating she said. Girl you are really noisy. All right I'll tell you I'm not going to lie to you which is I don't owe you any explanations. We were kissing. I'm tellin Ms. Tina. What can my mother say? I have 2 children so telling her wouldn't make a difference. I ain't talking about you kissing him. What are you talking about? His age, that man is 43 years old. So what I'm a grown woman now, I make my own decisions.

A crazy thought begin to float in Cheryl's mind knowing how mama is she probably would get in my business it was around 5:45 in the afternoon. Time was getting closer and closer she was very anxious to meet with Greg that evening even if they kissed again, like they did in the barbershop but when she did finally see him it around 8:00 in the evening he seemed a little worried as though something was bothering him. Which she did notice right away? Cheryl knew the minute she stepped foot in his gray-jaguar that had black leather interior seats and a booming system that was playing the song "caught up in a rapture" by Anita Baker she knew they were on their way to be alone and somewhere classy. He was quite talkative awhile they were riding. It wasn't classy enough when they pulled up in front of a tall brown apartment with foggy windows. It smelled like chicken feed inside, welcome to my castle he said. It wasn't a surprise to her that she was invited to a man's house this is something that usually happens. You have a comfortable place she told him. Which she was expecting a little more outgoing, and not his apartment. Make yourself at home.

Cheryl decided to take her shoes off and unbutton her blouse, wanting him to notice her. Are you hungry? Yes I could use a bite. You like pizza? I love pizza. Call Pizza Hut and order one to my address, and make sure you tell them with everything. Cheryl started licking her lips hungry as she was it was going on 10:30 and they were still waiting for the pizza, when the deliveryman finally showed up. He said the cost of the pizza was $11.00, Greg the pizza is here and the cost is $11.00. I'll be right out, oh I'm sorry man I was making a deal with one of the models I made famous, she was calling me from Japan he said bragging. It should not be $11.00. I thought it was a special. It is a special the guy said, but you was late too man. Here you go man. Cheryl was so embarrassed when the deliveryman left she couldn't believe Greg was complaining about how much the pizza cost, at that time she wanted to sneak and call a cab and leave here. He is fussing over $11.00 for a pizza when he has a nice apartment two cars a motorcycle.

That was telling her he was just down right cheap to spend money, Cheryl guess she wasn't worth it, which is usually most of the time with these men. They were sitting there eating their pizza and a glass of champagne laughing and talking enjoying this moment with each other, but he stopped eating his pizza and went to the bathroom to run some bath water. Cheryl wondered why he did that when he came out she asked him was he taking a bath because that was quite rude. No. I'm taking a bath he said. Well your pizza is getting cold I'm full he said. I wanna show you something as Cheryl walked towards the back of his apartment he guided her to where his bathroom was. Greg what are doing? I have a surprise. What is it standing there in the middle of his bathroom?

She couldn't believe what she saw a tub full of bubbles, where he gently took off her blouse which she had already unbutton a few buttons then took off her bra and unzipped her jeans, that was so tight it took her ten minutes to get them off. NO, she said, knowing this is what she wanted. Yes Cheryl, he started kissing her and she started kissing him. He gently moved his lips down to her breast sucking them like he had a baby bottle in his mouth; she yelled out as he picked her up and put her in the water. Cheryl put her, feet up in the air where the water faucets were, so when he came back into the bathroom he can see her body for sure. He couldn't resist her and she couldn't resist him. Reaching down to kiss her passionately. Greg, thank you for making me a bubble bath. No problem sweetheart anything for a queen he said. The way he kissed.

Cheryl hurried up and dried off with the towel as she came out of the bathroom Greg was in his bedroom lying there naked his body was oiled all over. Cheryl couldn't stop staring at his fine brown body and there they were non-stop making love half of the night. Cheryl then got angry when he put her in a doggy-style position, he smacked her on the behind saying fuck me, fuck me repeatedly, as she rolled over telling him to stop this it's not what she liked. Come on Cheryl let's have some fun. You are hurting me and I'm feeling a bit uncomfortable and dissatisfied. I'm tired Greg we been at it all night Cheryl said. When I take you home tomorrow will you be able to come to the shop. For what she said shaking her head nervously. I need to take some glamour shots of you for the portfolio. I guess that wouldn't be a problem. Whatcha you mean you guess I will probably have something else to do. I'm trying to make you a star. Right like you is a sho-nuff modeling agency. Did you know I made 15 girls fashion models to this day and there doing really well now, some of them is modeling for Ebony/ jet magazine. Ain't this what you want to do? Yes but I'm a bit shy about my body Cheryl said. Girl what are you talking about, you have a gorgeous body. I'm not really worried about that? What is it? It's not making it I'm worried about. Greg stood there saying nothing. Did you hear me? Yes I heard you; don't worry you goin to make it. Are you ready? Yes I 'm ready.

The telephone rang and he answered all nervous Cheryl hurry up and get dress, I'm meeting these people at the shop in the next 4 hours come on and make it snappy. Cheryl wanted to shout back but she was used to this kind of treatment anyway. What people are you meeting? Some modeling scouts. I'll see you at the shop later on this evening; will I have to bring some outfits? Yes that will be great come on I have to drop you off at the corner of Minnesota Ave. Why can't you drop me off in front of my house the same place where you picked me up from? Because I have met the people at the shop, now stop questioning me and get out and catch the bus, see you at the shop. Yeh I'll be there, Cheryl felt mad but anxious at the same time something told her to go and then on the other hand she didn't want to go, especially how he talked to her. When she got to the shop there was a lady there with golden- grayish hair grinning in Greg's face, and then he's flirting as though Cheryl meant nothing to him hey Darnell smiling, this is my ex-wife Pearl and this is Cheryl extending her hand out to shake her hand she didn't seemed much interested to shake Cheryl's. I don't shake women's hands.

Cheryl wanted to leave but then she thought about a modeling career. Greg, your ex-wife is not friendly at all. She just jealous, she stills wants to be with me she knew she had a good man and that's her problem she can't let me go. Don't pay her no mind come to the back with me, I need to talk to you the minute they went back of the shop he grabbed Cheryl and kissed her so passionately. Greg stop someone is coming back here, so what? Sure enough it was his ex-wife Pearl. Excuse me she said I didn't mean to interrupt you and your slut. Hold up Pearl, you don't know her well enough to be calling her a slut. Even if she did she shouldn't call me a slut in the first place Cheryl thought to herself. Maybe that's what I think of her she said. You can leave. Fine with me she said. I rather leave too Cheryl said. Don't go.. I don't like the way she talked to me. She's gone now so don't let her spoil our day. Now are you going upstairs with me or what?

When they went upstairs he starts biting on her neck like he was a vampire. I'm leaving she said. For what? You don't know how to caress a woman. When she got home her mama had this mean look on her face. Ma what's wrong? Are you fuckin that nigga down the street "huh" don't lie to me Cheryl and I know exactly where he works and tomorrow I'm going down there to tell him to stay away from you. He's too old for you and you have too many emotional problems to be dating somebody that old anyway. He's just taking advantage of you, a week went pass and Greg didn't call or accept any of Cheryl's calls she realized she fell deeply in love with him or she didn't know what love is. I don't care what mama said I going to see him regardless she thought. Ma what did you say to Greg it's been two weeks and he haven't call me or attempt to call me. Don't question me child that man is 44 years old. Cheryl felt angry with her at that time, she have feelings for Greg and her mamma blew everything now. She can't even model because of her no matter what she said she have to see Greg in person.

When she got there he acted as though he didn't see her. Greg, I need to talk to you. Go home Cheryl your mother made it very clear to me to stay away from you. Greg really hurt her feeling at that time she felt suicidal over this break up not only that Greg was ignoring her phone calls it had to be someone else he had in mind. She blames her mama for this, if she wouldn't stick her nose in her business. Cheryl guess it is her mamma's business she still living under her roof. Cheryl's mind was so bottled with revenge and anxiety she came down with a headache. She decided to go to her room and clean it up. I guess breaking up takes a toll on a person and it sure did take a toll on Cheryl. She need some time away from guys most of them want sex, some want security, and some want somebody to take care of them. She couldn't sleep so she went downstairs for a while to get a few peanut butter cookies and some orange juice, which a few hours later made her sick to the stomach. Nothing stopped Cheryl from waiting by the telephone, which that's something she normally won't do, the next day she saw Anthony.

Almost a year and they got into a altercation about how he haven't been visiting his daughter at the time they were near Greg's shop, and she was so angry she threw a bottle and it hit Greg's window which she didn't meant to vandalize his property, a couple weeks went pass Cheryl wanted to go pass the shop to say Hello, but thinking to herself that wouldn't be a good idea considering how Greg was mad at her vandalizing his property if he didn't know it was her, so she just kept walking until she caught the first bus where she was going to get Brian and Tylanya a winter coat before it really got cold outside. The minute she got off the bus a man approached her asking her for directions when she turned around she saw Greg driving down the street she finally crossed the street where the traffic was hectic the same man approached her again Miss can you help me and my partner out please, help you where? I have someplace to be Cheryl said angrily. Get in the car "bitch" I have a gun you better do as I say. Cheryl was so frightened then they grabbed her and put her in the car, one man slapped her in the face look "bitch" you have some money? No I don't shaking like a leaf. Don't lie "bitch" give me the wallet and get out. When they threw her out of the car she couldn't believe it, there she was shopping for her kids and these two men took all she had.

Cheryl had no other choice but to call Greg which she just saw him riding down the street as she saw Greg pull up she was so relieved, but afraid at the same time. What happen? He said sounded concern. She told him I was robbed by these two men one was a Jamaican and the other was a black man. How much did they take $263.00 in cash they took my wallet with all my important information in it. What's the big deal at least you're not hurt he said. When she got home she received a usual phone call. Hello still shook up from the robbery? This is Rasta-ma, asks Greg about your money? What did you say our boss Greg, you stupid "bitch" how do you think he can have this fake phony ass modeling agency? When she hung up she couldn't believe Greg put those men up to taking her money, Cheryl figure now he wasn't worth the tears,

Chapter 6

Up against the Wall

Day and weeks went by and all Cheryl could do was lay around the house. After Greg and her called it quits, in reality he stopped seeing her nothing mattered. She didn't even comb her hair her clothes was so raggedy looking, she didn't care who stared at her. Cheryl felt her life was over now her children mattered to her more then anything and now she can spend more time with which she did. Cheryl wanted someone to love and it seems like she keep getting involved with lousy men. Maybe one day I'll find Mr. Right whenever that will be she thought. She gotten so tired of lying around feeling sorry for herself she got up washed her face, brush her teeth, took a shower, something she haven't done in two days or so, considering how miserable, her body felt more drained so she lied down some more. She found herself falling asleep when she woke up it was morning around 8:00 she woke up staring out of her foggy windows watching the rain fall it was falling more and more the more the more it rained the more depressed she felt but this time she was getting up and do something for herself when the rain stopped, she decided to take a walk to Woolworth, this would really be depressing knowing that Greg's shop is just a couple blocks up from the store at that point she was undecided about this but she needed to get out a while so she put money in her purse taking the $7.00 I had to her name knowing damn well $7.00 isn't goin to buy nothing.

When she got to the store she did not know what to buy, so she picks up some lipstick, and an eyebrow pencil, and mascara, and couple boxes of summer's eve douche. A voice came from the other side of the lane, said may I help you miss? She really didn't know who this was referring to so she heard him say it again. Are you talking to me? Yes I am beautiful. Here we go again she thought, she yelled over to the other side and said I know what I'm looking for. I don't need any assistance form you thank you, in a harsh, but reluctant voice.

When he came from the other side he was tall- very light- skinned and was wearing a black uniform with Eastern shield on the patch of his shoulder. I see you stay fresh and all got two boxes of douche he said. That's my business and she kept walking up towards the cash register. Since these items were marked down Cheryl's wondering to herself will she have enough money to buy this stuff. When the cashier rung up the items Cheryl felt nervous thinking to herself, hoping this shit won't come over $7.00 it was $12.00, I'm sorry I have to put some of this stuff back on the counter I don't have enough money Cheryl said. The security came up and said how much is it? $12.00. Here's $5.00. Thank you and Cheryl walked out of the store she knew she wasn't so friendly to him but she was tired of letdowns. He probably ain't no good he just wants to have sex with me, and I'm not about to fall for the okkey-doke routine again she thought. He ran to the bus stop where she was can I take you out? No you cannot and thank you for the $5.00 you gave me I really appreciate. That's no problem baby. Let me tell you something you never ask a woman can you take her out, you always ask them their name first, by the way the name is Cheryl. My name is Mark can we exchange telephone numbers? I do have my own apartment. What does that suppose to mean? I just thought I let you know he says. You can feel free to call me anytime. Well, who said I was going to call you said Cheryl. Excuse me he said. No I'm just kidding, okay Mark it was nice meeting you I need to get, my bus it will be coming soon. Give me a call. I sure will.

On Cheryl's way getting on the bus she thought I should have gave him my number, it wasn't like we were getting serious she thought that he did give me $5.00 for my personal items that was nice of him he didn't even know me. It sure beats the hell out of putting those things back on the shelf. It's been three weeks, and Cheryl hasn't not call him, since she met him in the store. Cheryl got bold and picked up the phone to call him, but the whole conversation was based on the few bucks he gave her, he has his own place, he like staying home, she got to be bored somewhat the next day he called her and then she gave him her phone number. Hey, Cheryl how are you doing? I'm fine. I was calling to see what's up. His voice changed, when can you and me hook up? Tomorrow will be fine she was thinking. I can come over your house after I get off work. When? Is that around 6.00 ok? I'll let my mother know you will be coming over. After they got off the phone she was thinking what we going to do tomorrow talk, have sex, laugh, go to the movies that seems like the normal get up. She may as well look forward to this; because men are looking for sex that's their goal get a woman into bed and she means right away if they can. He's going to get a big disappointment if that's what he's after. Cheryl looking for someone to love her and respect her, so far she been getting dirt straight from the ground.

The cab pulls up in front of the house Cheryl couldn't help but to smile when she saw him. He looked so good even in his black uniform, he look so fine with his bowlegs. I though you never show up Cheryl said. I had to wash my dishes he said. So when will I see your apartment? Real soon would you like a soda or a glass of water? I would like a hug if you have that (Laughing) I have no problem giving you a hug as long as if that's all you're hinting around to said Cheryl. Something else are you uncomfortable with that because nothing is going to happen with you and I until I say it will. He starts laughing cut to the chase Cheryl I'm attracted to and you're attracted to me we're both adults, so what's with two people showing their true feelings. It just so soon you can understand that can you Cheryl said. Not really. What's wrong with a small kiss on the lips he said? He starts kissing her right out of nowhere she jumped up from the sofa where they were sitting, Mark we can't do this right now I barely know you. I'm not about to make the same stupid mistakes I've been making. What does that suppose to mean? It means I'm not ready. Come on girl you know you want me to put this sword inside you.

Cheryl immediately moved away from him and turned on the lights. She wanted to see his reaction once she saw his face he was sitting there with his penis straight out of his zipper. Mark you have to leave, we're two consenting adults stop playing games, and cut the bullshit. I want this to be perfect. Perfect for what? It's not like we're getting married or anything. I didn't say no such thing did I. Then what are you saying? I just think it's best we get to know each other better, as Cheryl moved her lips to tell him what's on her mind he gently slid his tongue into her mouth and kissed her, she was tempted but she couldn't. A man never kissed like that before as he kept kissing her she begin to tremble all over her body. I can fall in love with you girl. Don't say that, she felt loved just laying there with him watching T.V. and talking no sex and she really enjoyed that moment deep down inside. Cheryl felt like a cheap tramp it's only been a week since we seen each which she didn't call him for three weeks, after the foreplay they had sex for 15 minutes. She was sitting there wondering will he be man enough to call her again or will he tell her thanks for a nice piece of that ass of yours, or all I wanted was some pussy, or I don't want you girl. Cheryl was hoping that's not the case but if it is she would have to accept it, It takes two people to have sex. Going upstairs to wash up she smelled of old fish, as she went downstairs Mark was lying on the sofa sleep she wanted to wake him but he looked so comfortable so she slid up under the quilt, which she put on him so they won't get cold.

When we got up it was around 9:45 in the morning. Did you sleep well last night? Yeh I did with you next to me, I have to call you a cab before my parents get up. You're not just telling me that are you? Oh no. I meant why you ask? I'm just curious that's all she said. All right what's on your mind? Nothing come on you can talk to me. Okay if you wanna know it's just that men have been in and out of my life for the past three years. What happen? They don't treat me right. What makes you think I'm that kind of guy? When I'm with a girl I'm in for good. As he kept convincing her that he would be with he .You has nothing to worry about all right girly girl? I gotta get to work before it gets too late I'll call you on my lunch break. As she started towards the front door to give him a big wet juicy kiss. Her mama came to the door with her long flannel nightgown asking who's that nigga, another fuckin loser, mama he might be different, you do that every time you find somebody, they give you their ass to kiss, which she never lied and Cheryl couldn't argue with her on that note. She felt he was different from the others but when he left she felt sad. Cheryl could have stayed in his arms. She didn't want to fall in love with him her feelings are getting strong already.

It was 3:30 that afternoon Cheryl had not heard from him not since he left the house this morning at 11:00. Now she's getting worried what if something happen to him, his body could be laying on the side of the road or maybe her assumptions could be right, he don't want her that's all he wanted was her body. Cheryl knew it the minute he stepped foot in her door. Time was passing by so she decided to take a walk around the block but when she heard a few gun shots and then the police came speeding down the street she made a detour back to the house she wanted to call him but that would just make his ego high after he told her all those sentimental things, which by now she don't believe none of that bullshit he was talking. When she got back she couldn't stand it anymore she swallowed her pride and gave him a call. She got no answer that night. She tossed and turned lurking out of the window here I am, worrying about a man that I barely know she thought. She couldn't wait until she hears from him, a one-night stand that's all it was. She had to call his apartment again and this time a woman answered the phone now I see why he didn't have time for me she thought. "Hello" she said. May I speak to Mark? Hold on. Mark what's wrong I haven't heard from you in two days? I've been working. You still should have call. I'll let you go since you have company. No that's my sister. What's up tonight girl?" nothing" she said. Can you meet me in front of 7 eleven on Pennsylvania Ave? Why? Cause I think we need to talk. That evening she met him at the corner there he was standing there with a red shirt on a pair of blue jeans and some black flat dress shoes he even look better than he look in his uniform. She wanted to tell him off. But the looked so good to her, she just wanted to slob him down right then and there in front of the public but that wouldn't be lady like. She put all those good looks in the back of her head, so she got bold and asks him why was he avoiding her. I wasn't trying to duck. You didn't call or even attempt to call me why are you so dressed up? Are we going somewhere special? Hell no we going back to my place she really wanted to see his apartment see how he lives. They arrived at these projects call the Hopkins it was a mad house kids running through the bald grass, people sitting on the porch, drinking vodka, beer, people yelling across the street to one another. Drug dealers standing around the building waiting on a drug sale from addicts which is an everyday scenario. A quick exchange for money and poison that's what the drug ordeal was all about.

Cheryl look at all that chaotic stuff on the outside when they got in the inside his apartment it looked horrible she saw chipped paint coming from the wall his stove has not been cleaned for months his floors was dirty, the bedroom looked a little better than the rest of the apartment except for the play-boy magazine posters that were torn out of girlie magazine and posted up on the wall with hair grease. This was disgusting she thinking now how come his place looks like this with the job he has. It was getting kinda late after they sat down and talked thought she should call her mother to check in on the kids. He didn't think it would be a good idea. She is babysitting my children. So what he jumped up from the sofa now she is seeing the other side of him. She can tell he's really getting an attitude all because she wanted to call her mother as she was approaching the living room to use the phone; he kicked her in the stomach and then punched her in the chest with his hard fist she cried out. She kept telling him why are doing this holding her stomach shut up you ain't calling nobody he kicked her so hard she start vomiting on the floor. "Bitch" clean that shit off my mutherfucken floor. I need a mop. No I want to see you lick this shit up with your tongue. He started pushing her head towards the floor to lick up her own vomit. Cheryl didn't know what to do at that point, she needed to get home to her children it's almost 2am in the morning she went to use the phone, when she came back in the bedroom he was crying sitting on the edge of the bed saying he's sorry for what he did, Cheryl can't forget what happen please. I didn't mean it, by then the cab came blowing the horn outside we'll talk about it tomorrow she said. Please don't leave me I'm trippin right now. Since you trippin I'll give you sometime to get yourself together. You tried to make me eat my own vomit, if you care about, me you wouldn't force me into something so gruesome. I'll call you tomorrow. You leave me "bitch" I swear to God I will kill you.

Cheryl tried to get away from him but he kept insisting on yelling out of that broken window. Stupid of her to believe that he could be the right man she needed in life she thought to herself. Before she got to the corner so she can catch the bus he was running up the street behind her with a knife trying to stab her with it. Please I need to talk to you. Cheryl doesn't know what came over him. I need help I promise I will never lay my hands on you again no matter how hard he pleaded with her she just couldn't go back to him and give him another chance but then he made a promise maybe he's sincere at what he's saying. An hour later when she got home the telephone rang and it was Mark. She really didn't want to hear his voice right now. My sister is giving a house party tonight at her girlfriend's house in the basement. Why are you telling me?" That's nice" "don't be smart," I'm telling you cause I want you to go with me. I'll let you know in a couple of hours she said ready to hang up on him. No I need to know right now the party starts at 11:00 and it's already 7:45. I don't know Mark you hurt me. Please I'm begging you. All right I'll go. "Good." but if you do this again it's over and I mean that shit Cheryl said. We'll pick you up at 10:00 be ready.

When she hung up she hurried up and took a shower then she didn't know what she was wearing considering on such short notice. She don't have no business going anywhere with this maniac she wanted to look jazzy. As she jumped out of the shower to look through her closet realizing she didn't have anything to wear she just have to run over to East over Shopping Center to buy her something and since it's the first of the month and she just got her welfare check, which she spent practically the whole check on the kids at which that's the purpose of getting it for them it's their money, She only had $56.00 to spend on herself. Nothing to proud of receiving money from the government, she only standing on one leg right now, well, she would just do what she have to do, so she slipped on a pair of green sweat pants with this holey white t-shirt and pair of sandals. Since she didn't own a pair of tennis shoes there she was going from store to store to put a outfit together, but some of the shops were already closed. Marianne's was still open she decided to buy a one piece body suit and a black Zorro hat. Time was approaching fast so she hurried up and went home, to get dressed.

When Mark and his sister pulled in front of the house she stepped out with her black Zorro hat and body suit and a pair of four inch heels. They didn't know what to say she actually brought this outfit to make him jealous in case other guys were there, and the only reason why cause of his abusive actions. Cheryl thought I don't deserve what he has done to me. The whole time they were riding he didn't say a single word to her. She knew why she was shaking when they got there, she was afraid of what he might do. So she got a cup of juice and stood in a corner near the tool shed out in the yard. Hey girl putting his arms around her waist as though he's saying this is my lady, I won her don't fuckin touch her look at her and you better not touch. In other words, relating this message to the guys go and get something to eat this a party have a good time he said with this strange smirk on his face. Cheryl couldn't loosen up like she wanted to because everybody there was acting anti-sociable. At the moment she just wanted to get up and leave, except for this one guy that was trying to mack. Are you here with someone he said? Yes I'm here with my boyfriend. Who Mark? That crazy mutherfucker he ain't shit. But you'll see how this nigger is if you stick around long enough. Nice meeting you beautiful. She should have gave him her phone number just to find out what he actually talking about concerning Mark. Anyway, what happened the other night she shouldn't be so quick to tell people that's her man.

Cheryl looked in the trash can where they had the beers at; she went outside with a beer in her hand to try to mingle a little bit. No one was paying her any attention especially the women, they must be thinking she here to steal their man away but that was not the case. Because she was there with a man that abused her. She went back into the house to sit down at that time she was feeling uncomfortable. Now she was ready to leave she looked around the house to see if she can find Mark. She wondering now did he take off and leave her here with these strange people. She looked almost everywhere, she then went upstairs where he was standing in the hallway kissing some girl. Feeling her from her breasts to her vagina.

Cheryl tried to hide the hurt she was feeling but she couldn't, she broke down with tears running down her cheeks. She wish she never allowed him into her space. Cheryl tried to find the guy she met when she got there but he must have left already. Which she couldn't blame him cause this party was a drag. There he was coming downstairs as though nothing happened. Take off the hat Cheryl, you look too cool. Why? He then smacked it off her. That's why nobody ain't talking with your ass. Cause when I get 50 years old and your daughter will be 19, I'm gonna tear that ass up. You are a sick individual she said in an angry voice. Get the fuck out of my face. Not until I get my purse and bag I brought over here Cheryl said. Your not getting shit out of here.

As Cheryl started to leave his friend Jamie came over and his sister and her two sons was all sitting there laughing and talking as though they were sitting there waiting for Mark to hit her. She didn't care all she wanted to do was get as far away from this crazy lunatic, which she should have done much earlier in this so-called relationship. Cheryl really got nervous when she saw his son's mother walk through the door.

She saw the commotion going on, she told Cheryl that you don't know me and I don't know you, but Mark is a crack head. When she said that Cheryl had her mouth hung open no wonder he's been acting strange. By the time he was ready to leave his friend Jamie was in his bedroom talking about some drugs they trying to cuff. So Cheryl knocked on the door when he open the door they both grabbed her and ripped her clothes off and punched her in the face sprung her neck and they both raped her. Now she all distraught she had no other choice. Cheryl was running down Pennsylvania Ave, with barely nothing on. Bruised from head to toe, when the ambulance arrived they asked what happen? Which she did tell, there was nothing they could do but to take a report and advise her to press charges against those bastards. Of course nothing was done behind this incident she was so much in turmoil and pain she just hope he suffers the same way she did.

Chapter 7

Conniving

For more than three weeks Cheryl still felt ashamed of what happen. She thought it was her fault. If she would have got out of that rat-race awhile ago this wouldn't have happen. She woke up the next morning suffering from the pain she experienced. She was so angry at what those bastards did to her, they raped me, they beat me, and they tore my self-esteem down she thought. She didn't know how she was going to cope with thus turmoil after three weeks she was still emerging from her vagina. All she could do is pray that nothing like this happens again. That night the telephone rang and she couldn't believe it was Mark calling her as though nothing happen. What's up he says in a joking way? Why are you calling me after what occurred? I just called to see how you doin. Fine as long as you're not in my life. You ask for it "bitch". Don't ever call me again she said hanging up her phone. She didn't feel bad at all at what she did. Sitting in her room thinking to herself, I'm going to take care of my children and be by myself that's all they do is tell lies, use and abuse, and get you into bed, that's their main goal. Just to boost up their ego, I'm tired of it.

Cheryl was looking for a father for her children she guesses that's the angle or was she looking for love? She needed love which she had not received as of yet. As she was going into the kitchen that night she heard police sirens going off as though there was drug- raid or something, which there was a lot of officers bursting through the house a couple doors away. Sometimes she wonder why this country is is so corrupted. With some of the people in this world doing drugs, stealing, robbing, raping, murdering, lying, having an evil and hatred heart. If only she could do something, more about the situation she thought. Cheryl took a look at herself in the mirror and she started to wonder, am I good enough for these guys I met? Maybe I'm not.. She stayed up almost every night thinking about that night she know dragging over this is only going to make her a weak person. She just knows being with a man is not going to make her happy. She knew one thing she was the cause for her own happiness.

So when she got up the next morning she put on her sweat pants and a white t-shirt and grabbed a towel to go jogging. When Cheryl returned from her short run she was so exhausted she came in and fell right in her bed, as soon as she laid down her friend Nikki knocked on the door. "Hey Cheryl she started yelling her name come outside girl stop sitting in there feeling sorry for yourself. She just came in here from jogging she just feeling a little tired that's all she said. Well get your tall ass up and come outside, and please stop moping over that sorry mutherfucker. Nikki I'm not feeling bad over Mark, I'm just angry about what he did she said. Cheryl you have to let things go shit happens. That's not just shit I was raped not only by him but his friend too. Let's go outside on the front porch. "Fuck that shit" Cheryl said alright it's not going to be easy trying to forget the fact that I was raped. She feel so humiliated everybody knows about this. If you would have not told your business they wouldn't know nothing said Nikki. The minute they stepped out on the front porch people were coming from across the street asking Cheryl if she was okay.

All she wanted to do is tell them to mind their business and go back in the house and slam the front door right in their faces. Only reason she had that assumption was because she saw a lot of snickering and laughter. It was like she was being interviewed by news reporters there's nothing more than a bunch of noisy neighbors. After being questioned by those crazy neighbors of hers, she went into the house and put on this royal-blue dress that has been hanging in her closet for months. She didn't have much since she only had a $357.00 a month to survive off of. I don't know why in the hell I would put this nice ass dress on just to sit on the porch she thought. If it wasn't for Nikki pressing her to get some air she would just sit and cry. Maybe she right I do need to stop feeling sorry for myself Cheryl thought. But if she didn't aggravate me, I'll probably still would have been coot up in that stuffy room of mine.

As Cheryl sat there with Nikki all she did was think and stare out into the street. Cheryl "snap out of it." I'm sorry Nikki I just can't sit here and pretend like nothing happen, those two fools beat me, stuck their nasty penises into my vagina not only that, they tried to sodomize me she said crying out to her. Go and get some tissue and wipe your face just as Cheryl come back Nikki was standing there talking to these two dudes who pulled in front of the house in a burgundy barrette. One of them got out with a pair of rusty lookin jeans and a white t-shirt with bulging muscles. The other one was very tall and skinny. Cheryl come here she said. For what? Nikki I don't feel like talking to any men right now. But it's nothing wrong with having a conversation with anybody. How you doing Miss Lady they both said I'm okay. Why so sad? I was brutally raped Cheryl said. You didn't have to tell them that see that's why everybody knows your fuckin business. Well they asked me a question so I told them. See Cheryl you need to keep certain things to yourself now you see why you have so many problems. Do ya'll always argue like this? NO! She just wants me to forget about what happen and I can't just forget something so dramatic Cheryl said. Well it's nice to meet you guys I do have a lot of laundry to do. She don't need to do no damn laundry she's just trying to brush ya'll off. We not goin to keep you desirable looking ladies so we better get down the road. we didn't tell you ladies our names.

One guy said my name is Kevin the other name is Frankie, I 'm sorry that happen to you, some brothers don't know how to treat a young woman. Well that's the reason why I can't trust men anymore. You can trust me. Cheryl assumed he was trying to talk to her and she guess Frankie was trying to talk to Nikki. I'm through with men Cheryl said to Kevin. What you want a woman? Hell no I could never be with a woman, I'm just sick of men stepping on me like I'm some slut. I can dig it, so did you take that mutherfucker to court. No because they felt like I was lying due to the fact that he was my boyfriend, but it wasn't just him it was his friend too. So you're telling me his friend was in on this, too damn bad, that's terrible. I 'm worried as much because as that old saying goes what comes around goes around. So does this mean you're not interested in dating anymore? You got it she said, I don't have time to put my all in a relationship and I get hurt over and over again. But you shouldn't apply to all men; everybody is not the same he said. So far the one I came across ain't worth shit and I ain't about to put myself into another one. I'm tired of getting hurt it's not worth it Kevin it was nice talking to you I gotta get back into the house. I have a lot of things to do. Wait a minute uh what's your name again? It's Cheryl, look Kevin it was nice talking to you. Come on now can I get you telephone number and call you sometimes, maybe you'll feel better please I promise I won't pressure you into anything you're not comfortable with. See you're smiling don't let what happen keep you from shining girl. Okay I'll get a pen, laughing in a sarcastic way knowing he's talking bull-shit.

Listen Kevin I'm doing this because you seem like a gentleman these phone calls are strictly innocent. Deal as a matter of fact I'll call you on tomorrow around 7:00. As Cheryl went into the house to get a pen Nikki had sped off with friend Frankie. Your friend just kidnapped my friend, naw! He just took her for ride. She barely knows him I'm afraid something going to happen. Frankie is not that type of dude, I've been knowing him for 16 years, and as big as house, Frankie can't do much to her. That's not nice she said. Since Frankie left you here for a minute you're welcome to sit on the porch with me. That's fine would you like a glass of Kool-Aid? Yeh I'm kind of thirsty, anyway you got some Budweiser beer? No what would I do with beer I don't drink much only on occasions. That's good, you don't drink as much. I'm trying to quit, being around Frankie all the time all we do is ride down the Park and buy cases of beer he said. Here they come I'll call you tomorrow. See you later Cheryl said. Talking to Kevin made her feel much better realizing that all men ain't vicious and mean. She couldn't wait until Nikki got out of Frankie's car so she can tell her that Kevin and her exchanged phone numbers. Hey girl where have you been probably had sex? You were gone a long time. No girl why would you say that? Cause I know your ass you go from man to another man. I know you're not talking about men, some men acts nice to me, the ones I have not got involved with. Cheryl stop kidding yourself you always think these men want to be with you. If you think that than you're crazy. Than she said, Nikki you act like you know so much about men. I do more than you know, I've have some good men. I know you ain't talking about that bull-shit you was with. Why are you talking to me like that, you don't even have a man? Nikki said, I tell you one thing I won't go through some of the shit you went through, and why can't you hold onto a man. I don't feel like discussing that with you Cheryl said. Be quiet then face facts they don't want you, all they after is some pussy and you know it Nikki said. I'll talk to you later. Don't get mad. Tell me this what number did Kevin give you he gave you his sister's number with your Knave ass. Uh come on Cheryl wake the fuck up. And what do that suppose to mean it means? That means that mutherfucker ain't shit. Oh like you so damn perfect and never got dogged. No cause I'll kick a nigga to the curve. Bye Nikki, I'm going into the house.

Later that day she couldn't stop thinking about all the nasty things Nikki was saying but Cheryl couldn't let what she said bother her. She just wanted to break down and cry, and also she wasn't going to let her guard down neither. She just went on and ignored it and got herself ready for the next day. So she can see about this Security job tomorrow hopefully she would get hired. She really didn't want to work for Security Company because of the risks she would be facing. When she realized what time it was she had to rush to catch that next bus.

There she was standing at the Silver Spring Subway Station all nervous and shook up; this was the only job that she had to be face to face with a person. She really didn't know what to say so she would just go in that office and act like she knew the technique for an interview. Good morning she said to one of the managers in the office. Uh I'm here to see Mr. Pollack in the recruiting division Cheryl said. Have a seat and he will be right with you. You must be Cheryl glad to meet you come in my office, did you have a hard time getting here? Yes sort of, I had to ask for directions some people just kept walking she said. Why did I say that he didn't even ask me no such thing she thought to herself? Cheryl sat quietly before she blows this interview and the job she thought. So have you done Security work before? No she answered. Well since this company advertise no experience necessary all I need for you to do is get a police clearance. Which is a background check, pick up your uniforms tomorrow afternoon around 3:00 that's when our shipment will be here. Cheryl was so overjoyed about working again even though she'd be wearing a uniform with a knight stick. She couldn't wait until she got home so she can tell her mama she got a job. So now she can get out of her mamma's house and get on her own. Cheryl could have her own space and some company.

Cheryl called Kevin to tell him the good news. The only thing she hated was Kevin only gave her his work number and not his home number. When she called his job she asks him why? Just before she dialed his number the phone rang and it was him. She couldn't wait to tell him about her new job. I don't know why he's not my boyfriend and never will be she thought. Kevin was into Culinary Arts he worked at Union Station as a Cook, later on that day he came over with some chocolate chip cookies wrapped in some aluminum foil. Cheryl smelled the aroma from the cookies on his way upstairs to her room. I see you have some cookies. I brought them for you. That was sweet of you; early today when I spoke to you I forgot to tell you I have a new job as a Security guard I start next Tuesday. I'll be working on different contracts. That's good what's your hours? It varies because of the agencies, I'm kinda afraid of working security. Why is that? It's just that people get feisty and irritable when you try to tell them what they can do and can't do; I just have to do my best and don't get stressed out by people. So Cheryl what are you doing tomorrow? Nothing, same ole routine as usual. Wanna have lunch? Sure. Well, I'll see you tomorrow; I gotta get up early and feed these hungry people. I guess working around the public can be frustrating it's a headache that's what it is she said. I can't wait until I find another job. I better let you go we both have a busy day. I'll see you tomorrow beautiful.

As Cheryl went back into the house she begin to wonder, is Kevin gonna let me down just like the rest of those low-life I had in my life, I hope not that's not the case, because if so then it must be something about me that men is only interested in is my body. It would be nice to get married one day. Cheryl was some what happy about having lunch with him, she will get a chance to talk to him and see what he's up to. What he has to offer, which is probably nothing like the rest of them dirt bags. I had better get ready for dinner she thought. But she couldn't decide what to wear. As she walked downstairs to see who was knocking at the door it was Kevin with a foam-plated tray of chicken wings and fried rice from a Chinese carry-out. Cheryl held her mouth open for so long, actually disappointed that he couldn't take her out like he promised to do. So here she is dressed up in a white sleeveless dress. Look at you he said all dressed up. YES! Look at me she said sounding mad. Why are you all decked out? Well, I thought we were going out to eat instead you bring me food. Who got that kind of money he said. Anyway thanks for the chicken and rice. And here is some cookies they were in my jacket. Cheryl I can't stay I have to make a run, so I'll call you later. I have to work tonight. I guess I will talk to you tomorrow.

As she watched him run out of the house to get into his car, she wondered why he has not called me from his sister's house where he suppose to live. Which she don't believe. The next morning when she came home from work she fell fast asleep from the long dragged out night. But as she was lying there she felt someone kissing her in the mouth. She looked and it was Kevin with a plastic bag full of those staled cookies he always brings her over and over again. I sure hope this is not what he brings a woman for a gift trying to get into my good graces she thought. Because she would be disappointed if all he has to offer is some damn cookies, which he stole from the job. "Wake up sleepy head. I'm up. She was tired; they really worked the hell out of her last night. I'm really going to be tired tomorrow the convention center is sponsoring a car show. You know it gets crowded. Yes my boss told me it can be hectic at times so get plenty of rest. Yeh I have to work 16 hours tomorrow, I'm not gonna keep you since you have to work. Cheryl I need to ask you something, but I don't know how to ask you. Go on, I'm listening. Can we meet somewhere after you get off work? What's up with all this meeting jive it's getting on my nerves? Why can't I meet you over your sister's house where you suppose to live? No she's out of town. Shouldn't it be obvious to meet there? I don't have a key. You don't have a key? My sister is a nag; she'll give you a headache. What do that have anything to do with you having a key to where you reside? She ain't giving no nobody a key not even her own kids. So back to what we were discussing where do you want to meet me at? Down the street at the corner supermarket. See you then. As soon as he left the phone rang "hello. Cheryl whatcha doing this Nikki long time no see. I thought you were upset with me? I guess that's why I have not heard from you. I'm not mad at you girl. I got something to tell you Cheryl. Do you know Kevin lives with a woman? No he doesn't you're just saying that. Kevin told me that Frankie just fucked you and never called you again; I figured you called me all because you got screwed around. I ain't worried I wasn't interested in him. Anyway listen to me Cheryl that man lives with a broad up there in East Gate Projects. That's bull-shit he lives with his sister. Believe what I tell you she said, giggling on the phone. Well I'll call you tomorrow and ask him. Who told you this anyway? Frankie told me the first time we met each other. Why didn't you tell me this in the beginning? Cheryl how I suppose to know ya'll was getting serious. We're not serious and that's beside the point Nikki you suppose to be my friend. Friends don't keep things like that a secret. Cheryl I'll call you back I have another call. Okay bye.

When Cheryl got off work she was so exhausted she didn't feel like doing anything, but when Nikki told her he lived with another woman she felt like the whole world caved in on her. After all she been through this is one thing she didn't need to hear. Considering the length of time Kevin and her started dating even though they haven't got intimate he seems like a nice guy. Like the rest of them seems nice, and then monsters, and liars. She felt special and that means a lot to a person. Over and over she kept hearing Kevin lives with a woman, she couldn't release the anger she felt she couldn't understand why he didn't her tell this. As soon as she hear from him she going to let him go, cause she had been through enough. The more she thought about it the angrier she got, she got up from the couch that she was sitting on and stormed right out of the front door onto the sidewalk and stood there for a couple of minutes. She got so mad and she wanted to walk to where he lived and knock on his door and smack his damn face for wasting her time, but that would make matters worst.

That evening he called Cheryl and asked if she could meet him there at Eastgate when she got there he was standing beside a brick wall with graffiti written on it. Hey lady, what's wrong he said? Ask your woman what's wrong. My woman who told you some shit like that? Does it matter who told me? Ask you friend who said it? How come you didn't tell me? Cheryl I don't own you any exclamation we ain't involved, I haven't fucked you yet. And these lies you told you will never have sex with me. Can't we still be friends? I don't think that would be a good idea. Look Cheryl I was gonna tell you but you probably wouldn't talk to me no more. I'm leaving her anyway. Oh please, who do you think you're talking to a fool? How long have you been with her? Seven years. If you haven't left her all this time you will never leave her. Don't leave on the count of me. You're wrong if you thinking that Cheryl. Okay I can prove it to you, better than I can tell you. Tomorrow be ready to ride with me over my sister's house. Better yet I'll pick you at 6:00, Kevin do me a favor before you cause more problems.

When Cheryl got home she was still upset so she called in and told her boss she wasn't working tonight. So she went into the bathroom and ran herself a hot tub of water she easily slid her aching tired body into the water. When she got and dried off she heard a horn blowing outside, she then went over to her window to see who was calling her. It was it was him standing beside his beat -up Toyota yelling her name as loud as he could. She hurried up and slid on something and went to see what he wanted. Cheryl really meant what she said to him, later that evening she agreed to go over to his sister's house with him. Now it was a big mistake when she got there his sister told her that he has genital herpes. Cheryl really could not understand why would she go against her brother like that all because he owes her money? She met Nikki through Kevin and Frankie, she mentioned that Nikki's friend Veronica, is sleeping with Kevin they all hooked one night that I was not around. She not your friend she told me, she talks about you like a dog. At that time Cheryl told her it was nice meeting her and she left and caught a cab. She knew then she needed to get away from Kevin before it get out of hand. She was glad that they never got sexual. And with friends like Nikki who needs enemies.

Chapter 8

Pitiful

By that morning Cheryl didn't feel much like going to work. Considering today the company were sponsoring the car show at the Convention Center she better go. So she went downstairs to pour herself a cup of coffee, since she did not have enough time to fix breakfast cause she had to work at 9 am. She gathered all her belongings together rushing out of the door so she could catch the bus. So she can get to this underpaid job which she can't complain, it's better than waiting on a welfare check. Now Cheryl feels independent and responsible, as soon as she save enough money she will be moving out of her parent's house. Which she needed to get away from here as soon as possible. Before she can get halfway down the street she realize she forgot her night-stick. Which she know that crazy supervisor Brown is going to act like a jack-ass. She really ain't in the mood to hear his yelling.

Now she had to hurry back to the house to get it, she got one foot in the door before she heard ya late. Let me explain Brown. Okay I wanna hear this one. You won't believe this but I left my night-stick and I had to go back to get it. Yeh right saying it in a sarcastic voice okay then put your bags up and sign-in and get on post. Where at on post? You'll be assigned where the Pontiacs are, and tomorrow you will where the BMW's are. So get to work, for two weeks that is where you be for now, do you understand? Yes sir. One more thing don't let customers sit on top of the cars cause if my boss come by here and see you're allowing them to sit on these cars your job and my job will be in jeopardy. Now take your fine self downstairs and do your job. But Brown what if they don't pay me any attention. That's when you bring the situation to me, and I'll take care of it you're the boss, 10-4 she said. Feeling like saying can I go home for the rest of the day? She need a radio. Cheryl you beginning to be a pest. Sorry Brown I didn't realize I was getting on your nerves Cheryl said. Alright go the office and ask Jack to give you one. Now she's ready to go on post, should have been ready.

The minute she walked around the corner she noticed a customer sitting on top of a car. As bad as she got on his nerves she didn't bother calling him for this. Cheryl kindly asked if they could not sit on the vehicles. She didn't even bother informing someone was sitting on the car. So she sat there and said not a word, as time went by she was getting hungry she knew she had to work a double shift it was getting closer to 11:00

and the crowd was leaving she have not eaten all day and now it's time to punch out. She couldn't leave her post until somebody came to relieve her, this was hectic and she couldn't wait until 11:00. As Cheryl walked over to the booth to pick up a magazine they had on display shelf, here comes that nagger Brown. How's it going Cheryl? Well 12 hours is a long time to not have a lunch break. You're the third person who mentioned that to me, as soon Jack get his ass off the telephone I'll call Dominos to order a couple of boxes of pizza's. And whose suppose to pay for this pizza one employee said? The company is paying for it Darlene watch your smart mouth Brown said. I'll be glad when Jack is off the phone cause my stomach is growling Cheryl said to Brown. Are you Hungry? "Hell yeh" I been here just as long as everybody else she said. Tell me something Cheryl how old are you? Why? I'm just curios that's all? Okay promise you wont laugh' I'm 20. That's it? Really sounding, he said surprised I thought you were around 25. "Ooh "that's an insult she said. Check and see if Jack is off the phone. They sitting here shooting the breeze while their waiting on the pizza. Tell me your age. 27 I thought you were older than you appear to be, you're kinda young to be a head-supervisor of this company. Listen to this when I came to work for this company I worked four months and then became a supervisor. It's all in how you present yourself, and come to work on time and do the best you can do. Most of all it will get you ahead in this company or any company you apply for have a pleasant attitude. You wanna be a supervisor? No I'm interested in computers, or acting or maybe writing a play. Sounds interesting. Go tell the Delivery man to bring the pizza to the east wing of the building. I can handle that. She knew they ordered ten boxes; she couldn't wait to dig her hands in that box.

After going back on post, she was feeling tired so she shook herself so she won't fall asleep. Cheryl looked down at her watch she realized it going on 11:00 she immediately grabbed her purse so that she can punch out. But before she went upstairs to the office she called Brown to tell him, Officer Green is ready to clock out when she turned around someone said that's my last name too. So what she said sounding harsh she really didn't feel like talking or anything else. That's a coincidence, what's your name by the way? It's Cheryl, look I have to go I worked 16 hours and I don't feel like hearing that off- the wall bull-shit. Okay miss evil I was trying to be polite. Well you're polite at the wrong time. I'll let you go then. You have no other choice tired as I am she said. Definitely not her type, red lips and a gigantic head.

Finally, on Cheryl's way home to get some rest she surely needed. Cheryl's Mama had the radio on full blast all she heard was "let's get it on" by Marvin Gaye so then she knew rest was out, after awhile she lowered the volume some, when she did, Cheryl rushed upstairs to get in her bed. By the time she got up it around 10:00 in the morning, and today she have to work a midnight shift. She then spent time with her kids and before long she had to get ready for work again. Cheryl wanna be on time cause she don't need to hear Brown mouth again. She was not in the mood to hear his yapping. When she got there she was 20 minutes late, which she isn't. Brown was in such a good mood, Cheryl get on post sweetie. She couldn't believe it, he's not fussing it must be a good night, but then she took a good look at him his eyes were blood shot red. Then I thought, no wonder he's been smoking reefer. Now she know he's not gonna come around to her post and check on her every two minutes, which he normally do.

Maybe she can read a book no one comes in here overnight anyway. That wouldn't be a good idea she would lose out on getting a raise which she needed. This job is somewhat less difficult. Looking around the corner Brown smiling and chewing gum at the same time. Why are you in a chipper mood tonight? Laughing, whacha talking about Cheryl? And what's so funny? He said it's just that I never seen you in a good mood before you're always so touchy. Hold that thought, Cheryl I'll be back. Come back Brown I want to talk to you. As he walked away he looked back at her and smiled. Cheryl hopes he didn't get the wrong impression and if he did it wouldn't be a big deal anyway. That didn't take long I see you brought me back a soda. Hope you like coco cola. Yes my favorite just a little too much acid, I see you're sobering some. Shhh! don't say that too loud Jack might hear as noisy as the crazy mutherfucker is. That man is nosey next thing you know he'll go back to the office and tell Chris he overheard an employee say I was intoxicated. Chris be down my back for some shit.

Well, when I met her for the position she seemed stringent in so many words. She seem nice at times but don't let your guard down cause she will fire your ass in a heart beat. If I call her for some uniforms she answers the phone in a pleasant voice Cheryl said. Listen to me again don't let that lady fool you, put it like this everybody have their days can't argue with you on that. Some days I feel like I rather not be bothered. Cheryl you know I never saw you take a nap. That's not my job to sleep I'm here to work. And besides so you can scream at me. If you tired then you tired, you know what I'm saying. You can get some rest I don't mind he said. Oh here it goes again I know he's interested in me Cheryl thought. Which she hoped not she's not ready for this again, it's flattering. Can I ask you something? Why do you always come around and sit with me on my post? I enjoy talking to you, there's gossip going around about you. What gossip? That you're a male whore and you will screw every girl you see that comes to this company. I'm not even dating nobody work here or even on the outside. Who' been spreading these rumors? I rather not say, actually I heard the guy upstairs that does the schedule of the upcoming events talking about it Cheryl said. He doesn't even know me, I don't pay these folks no attention don't listen to the rumors another thing, whenever they see somebody new and they think they don't have a chance, then you're a "slut". You're telling me just because no one wants to jump into the sack with them you're a whore? You got it, this actually funny to me. I can ignore it .Whatever you do don't go to bed with none of these bammers, cause if you do your name will be all over this building. That's one of my least worries I'm not interested in any of these men said Cheryl. She couldn't help but to worry. She had a date with Pete one of the Convention Security staff members. Cheryl couldn't tell Brown it was none of his business. I'm a grown woman and it wasn't like I was marrying the man she thought. He did warn me about them. What's a little riding around and talking unless I get turned on which I doubt it very seriously I haven't been with anyone since Mark she thought. The next day Cheryl went to work there goes Randall with his big head and that gayish voice of his "whatcha doing" he said grinning? Sitting on my post somewhere you need to be, I'm floating right now, how come you can't be bored like the rest of us she said? I must float he said those are the rules. Oh well if it's coming from Brown then I guess you're right. I need a walk man to listen to. Oh I see you're a music lover. You got that one right. I 'm a jazz listener myself. I love all types of music hip hop, gospel, jazz classic reggae you name it. Are you into the back of the day music? Yes I am she said. I have lots of oldies like Chaka Kahn Maze, Patti Labelle. Really, I need to record some of your music, why don't we do this? I'll bring some albums over to your house. Sure that will be fine. When would you like for me to come over? Say Friday that's the next time I'll be off. What time? 6:00 that evening. As Friday approached Cheryl was so relieved to have the day off. She went downstairs and fixed her some fried chicken, potato salad and glass of fresh lemonade with a slice of lemon and then flopped into her daddy's favorite recliner and put her tired feet onto the foot proctor. Damn it felt good sitting down and resting for a change, and chair was so comfortable. No wonder daddy fussed at us when we sat in his chair she thought. Well I guess I better sit as long as I can before he gets home from work cause if he see me sitting here I won't hear the end of it she thought.

It was going on 5:30 now she have to hurry up and get dressed before Randall get here not only that, Pete is picking her up at 11:00 tonight as she got upstairs to pull her mini-blinds to her window there was Randall walking up the walk way with a hand- full of albums. I hope he doesn't think I'm recording all night long because I have a date she thought. Hi Randall I see you made it, also you made it with those high waters on too. You're funny you know that he says. Come on as they both approached the railings to the stairs Cheryl's mama opens the door and says in a loud tone "hold up". What's up? Like where are you going? Oh ma this Randall he brought some albums for me to record some music. You tell somebody something first before you tell somebody come over here and make a move up the stairs. My husband pay rent here not you. Thinking to herself I help pay bills to but that don't matter to her, at times since I'm the black sheep of the family anyway. So the next time you want to have company you ask me she said. Okay ma it's no need to embarrass me. What you mean so not to embarrass you this is my damn house witch. Come on Randall I don't have a lot of time I'm going out tonight. With who? A few girlfriends of mine. Doesn't matter, that's none of my business. You shouldn't ask. I mean you and me barely know each other and you're asking me questions. But why not get to know each other. I have no problem with that Randall, but you never question anyone especially someone you hardly know. Yeh! You're right sitting there nodding his head. It was getting late and she knew Pete and her was going out the last thing she need is for Pete to see Randall sitting here. Even though she's not interested in neither one of them. The only reason Randall is here so she can record those albums.

Randall we should wrap this up I do have a date, I guess Randall ain't so talkative since I told him I have a date she thought. Which she said she was going with the girls tonight. Are you finish recording yet I have one last song as the song. Randall grabbed his records in such a rush as though he wanted to leave. I'll see you at work Randall. I don't wanna ruin your evening don't say that, I want to get dressed and shouldn't be in my bedroom while I'm putting on my clothes. Now that would be disrespectful don't you agree? No he said as he started towards the steps almost falling. I should have known you would say no. I'll walk you to the bus stop. No need for that, I'll see you tomorrow at work. As she watched him out of her window struggling with those old rusty records she couldn't wait until he caught that bus so that she can get dressed. she didn't know what exactly what to wear so she just put on a pair of blue jeans and her red blouse she had for months and barely wore.

When she went downstairs Pete was standing against the car looking sneaky whatever it is it's not going to happen she thought. Hi how you doing? I'm fine. Ready? Yeh I'm ready. Grab your overnight bag sweetie. For what she said. We were going out to dinner, I checked all the restaurants in town nobody had any available seats. Cheryl realized what Pete said about grabbing a bag knowing all along dinner was out, but then she knew what he had on his agenda .she couldn't understand why they just couldn't go somewhere else, they didn't have to have reservations in Chinatown you can go there and sit down and order your food. As she grasped for air over and over she kept telling herself hopping in the sack was all these men had on their minds. Mainly this routine anyway at times which she feel so desperate to be with them but not being loved. When we pulled up to a big brown four story home in downtown D.C. the building looked some odd old the steps were made of brick and the railings going up to the front door were falling apart. There was an old man rocking back and forth in this rusty green swinger she was hoping he was visiting a friend, but it was not the case at all. Is this where you live Pete yeh this is home why are you coming to your house? She had to come to grips with herself she knew why they end up here. Just to watch some TV. If I wanted to watch T. V. I would have stayed home, she said hasty. Asking why we are here was sounding ridiculous knowing he wanted sex from her. Not at all he said. As she thought long and hard about what he had on his mind a tear started to run down her face. What could she do she had no way back home she left her money at home. which was stupid as they walked up stairs to where his room was she paused, she started to shiver a sad shiver, a cold shiver, a shiver that she knew she was being used and abused.

She was scared and frighten hoping and praying he wouldn't force his self on her. This was strange and creepy especially, this old house. once they got upstairs and he opened his bedroom which made of chipping wood the door knob had fell off they were in the room for only five minutes and he begin to strip down to barely nothing this brought a sharp pain in Cheryl's chest. Ain't you goin to lay down beside me? No I'm not sleepy. Come on girl. But you have no clothes on she said. I know this is how I sleep. as she sat on the edge of the bed listening to this bared-faced lie, she felt his hand reaching up inside her blouse unloosening her bra strap as his warm hand kept reaching and touching where her breast were. Cheryl felt a warm sensation and again she tried to resist him, but then she didn't like the way he touched her. Made her feel miserable and sad, unhappy. After this was over her heart felt like it dropped to her feet. Wishing she could run straight out of this disaster and would end up in the middle of nowhere trying to keep her composure was really hard to do. Am I hard up for sex Cheryl thought, because this was nothing but sex and lust? He didn't even offer me anything to eat, so desperate and anxious how could I do this with someone I barely knew she thought. Was this loneliness she felt? This getting to boring I think you should take me home Cheryl said to him. As she walked to the bed picking up her clothes where he was still lying down at. Are you ready? Yeh I better get you outta here I have a important date tonight, oh did I mentioned that I'll be going back to Ohio next week. No you didn't, listen Pete you don't have to explain to me. I know what you wanted from me. What do you mean by that? This was a quick, dry, lazy, fuck she said. since you put it like that then get your clothes on so I can drop you off in front of those projects you live in. you didn't have the nerve to ask me if I wanted dinner or not Cheryl said. This not my pay week, and you didn't eat before you came out? It don't matter if I eaten or not what I see you're nothing but a down outright cheap skate. Nowadays you can't show a lady a nice time. You call this a nice time? Look I'm ready as soon as you are.

Cheryl got out of the car she slammed the door as hard as she can when she got into the house she went into the kitchen to make herself a cup of coffee. Forcing herself to take sip after sip after this awful date some date no dinner no conversation I guess that's what one night stands are all about. This will be my last miserable date she thought. The next day she went to work she felt like shit, she didn't feel much like socializing with anyone. Cheryl felt like a low-down slut, after what she did with that no good bastard no one said much to her at that time except stared at her as though she was a piece of trash. Actually that's the way she felt considering her promiscuous ways. When she noticed eye glancing she knew she had a reputation here which was not good in the workplace. As she walked down the hallway of the convention center swinging her nightstick after a few hours, she began switching as though she didn't care what they thought, which she did. She then notices a few of the cleaning crew were shaking their heads. Two of the ladies in the administrative desk were whispering in each other's ears. Cheryl saw Brown shaking his head coming toward her. I need to see you in the office, as she followed Brown grasping for air, she knew at that time what he wanted to discuss with her. There she was trotting upstairs behind him as though she was a child coming to get some candy.

Well Cheryl I know you're wondering why I call you to my office he said with a worried look on his face. I have a pretty good idea what this meeting is all about. Please whatever you do don't go out with any of those

Convention officers. Why is that? The word is all over the entire building it was said that you went over Paul's house. You mean Pete. It's Paul; see he didn't even give you his real name. It doesn't matter anyway it meant nothing Cheryl said. Cheryl that guy told everybody he fucked you and you spread your legs so wide he could run a 24 footer in your ass. Then said he dropped you off at some dirty projects in S.E. watch out for those guys. But I told you it was nothing Cheryl said. A week later the rumors didn't cease everybody kept talking. It was nothing Cheryl could do nothing. She felt low, sleazy, trashy, the next few weeks she tried to avoid everyone by doing her job and tending to her business. Her reputation had been ruined the only thing she could do was resign, but that wouldn't be a wise decision considering she had two children to raise. That evening she went to work sitting there on her post, here comes Randall with this aggravated look on his face.

Cheryl wanted so badly to ask him what the hell was he staring at. Hey how you doing in such a cheerful voice he said. After seeing a dreary look on his face. Not good. What's the matter? Oh as though you don't have not a clue? Oh come on Randall I'm sure you heard the rumors that's been floating around in this building. About you? Yes about me. Don't pay them any attention. Do you really think those punks getting under my skin? Randall I rather not discuss this any more. I just wanna forget about it, I guess this mess put a damper on me asking you for your phone number. No it didn't I'll give it to you. Here is mine she said. Here is mine, he said with excitement. So for the next couple of days they talked on the phone for hours at a time the conversations were interested, but then he wanted her to come over to meet his family. Actually she wasn't ready for that but then she went over to meet his grandmother and his niece. which they seem to be quite friendly as she looked around the house she could tell it was quite bad it looked demolished with old raggedy looking carpet there was old paintings on the living room wall. With dusty antiques the railings going upstairs was falling off. Cheryl then checked out the rest of the house where his room was, she felt uncomfortable trotting upstairs his room was filled with old classic albums mirrors on the wall where his bed was it seems to be an attic instead of a room. The bed had springs coming from edges of it, with dingy sheets that had not been changed in weeks the looks of it. She wanted to say something nice about his house. So she kept quiet it had a smell like a old folks home by his grandmother being the age she is, she guess that was the reason for the smell.

As Cheryl glanced over at him he seemed to proud of his home, she then thought to herself she had no room to talk besides, she lived in the projects, although they do clean their house. They went to his back yard, and the dogs they had in their yard had defecation all in the grass area. She wanted to get out of there the smell made her nausea to the stomach. After seeing that foul smelling place she got hungry, she started hinting around like she going to the store to get a bite to eat as she was rubbing her belly, Randall asked if she wanted a cheeseburger with lettuce, tomatoes, onions, she immediately said sure. So he went into the kitchen to stir it up hopefully it wouldn't take long. Knowing they both had to be at work 6:00 and it was after 4:30 after they ate the burgers he started talking about upstairs knowing that was the oldest trick in the book she sat on the couch. he reached over and took her hand into his, at that time she was so nervous and they kissed so passionately the way he kissed her it was long where is she needed some air, that was a kiss she wished for. Before she let things go any further, she pushed him away from her, if I give in I would regret it, I don't need to. This would only push my reputation into a deeper situation Cheryl thought to herself. After she rejected Randall he barely spoken two words to her on their way to work. Deep down that kiss turned Cheryl on. She was shaking and shivering all the way there. When they got to work she told Randall not to spit a word of this to no one and indeed he didn't. Just before she got to her post one of the convention center officers called out hey freakin bitch Paul ripped that pussy up didn't he?

Cheryl turned around and got really mad then words started coming from her mouth like they never did before. She quickly went outside to grab anything she could get her hands on. That would only make matters worst she thought. As she kept thinking about what he said she went over to a bench to sit and get over her anger. she saw a log she rushed inside that building to hit him with it at that time she could cared less about that job she couldn't release her anger her thoughts were telling her to leave this job you don't need this embarrassment here you can find work someplace else after she thought about it she stormed straight to Brown office to give him a two week notice that she would be leaving CES Security for good. When he asked her why she was leaving she told him she didn't feel comfortable here, this place is no where to work. After she relieved all that stressed that was built up inside of her, she then told Brown she was just upset about the situation. I don't know Cheryl, Chris talked to the head Supervisor and he told her what happened the next day.

Cheryl received a phone call from headquarters saying that she wasn't eligible for unemployment benefits and she was immediately terminated from the company because was about to commit a crime by doing bodily harm. Now unemployed again, she regret allowing that dumb ass to get on her nerves. She had two children to support the next couple weeks she was depressed. She couldn't eat, sleep. Nor jog. Cheryl was devastated she had been deserted all because of some gossip. She called back and try to convince them that it was a simple mistake she was angry, but the head recruiter told her no she cannot return back to CES under no circumstances. After she practically beg for her job back, she felt suicidal this was it, useless, distraught, no hope, despair, this is her last chance. She have to get away so she walked up to the corner store to buy some Tylenol to end all this depression. She called everyone she could think of even a psychiatrist no one seem to care; no one listened to her problems. She had to sit down and think for a minute she can't do this she have two beautiful children who needs her. She's their mother, father, counselor their supporter, role model, what the hell am I doing, this isn't right I could never forgive myself for even trying such punishment, nor will her children. Who would they turn to she thought to herself?

She would have to keep her composure the next few days she went roaming through the newspapers calling employment agencies. She received nothing, no calls, not even an interview this was frustrated but she knew she couldn't give up. this kinda stuff made her somewhat lazy sitting at home eating cupcakes, potato chips in a month's time she gain a lot of weight, so she started her twice a week routine by jogging and eventually she begin to loose weight as she came back from a 20 minute run Randall called wanting to know how she was doing. Coping she told him, not working bothered her a little but not much. Maybe getting away from CES was the best thing for her. Another job will come along soon and things would start to be bright for her and hopefully she will have her own place. Well I'm not going to hold you he said, yes I need to take a shower you see I'm sweaty from the run. Oh you jog I like to jog to. Give me a call later on that evening.

He called again hello he said in a such a sweet sounding voice. I see you stuck to your word Cheryl said. Yeh uh Cheryl? Yes I'm listening. I called early to ask you something but I was afraid. What is it Randall are you shy? A little. Since you called spilled it out on me? I wanted to ask if you wanna go out sometimes. I don't know yet I have to think it over. Okay? I'm a patient man I can wait. No one has ever said anything to her in that way before when Randall and Cheryl hung up she was in complete shock. Ever since Randall and Cheryl's first semi-date he's been calling and asking to come over again every time he asks she would have an excuse. Because she didn't want to get hurt he seemed to be a nice guy and all, it was all to soon to get intimate with him but that didn't stop him from calling her everyday. He would call just to say hello at times it became a shock to Cheryl to see someone can be that patient. After she gave it some thought the next day he asks her about coming over. I might just do that, but I'm not ready for any let downs she said. Which Cheryl knew in the back of her mind she was in for the rapture.

A couple days later each time he called he never mentioned a word about coming over. At that time Cheryl had got impatient he was at least calling twice a day she didn't care anymore all she wanted was to be touched. After a week went pass it finally happened after three and a half months it was a good feeling, a nice feeling, he didn't put a rush on being intimate with her. Everything was fine until one evening they were supposed to meet each other, standing on Pennsylvania Ave. she stood there for over an hour but no show from him. So then Cheryl went back home she called his house to find out what was the hold up when his grandmother answered the phone, she sounded a bit harsh Cheryl asked her where he was. She said she did not know but then she heard some devastating news about him. She said he had a drug-habit this was awful. Cheryl didn't know what to say after hearing something as shameful as that that. When she finally heard from him he told her he was robbed and that was the reason he didn't call because he had no money to take her to the movies. She couldn't hold in what his grandmother told her it was like a bomb dropped on her head. "Randall there is something I need to ask you. Your grandmother told me that you have a drug-habit. Don't believe nothing she says she has all-timers disease, no baby that's not true. Alright I'll settle for what you say what made her tell me such of thing? As long as they kept talking about this Cheryl was getting angrier by the minute. He said Okay. I'll talk to you later I have to get the kids ready for a birthday party.

Thanksgiving approached the following week and Cheryl began to get excited but then she was confused on where she was having dinner her mama is preparing dinner at home and so is Randall and his family. She knew if she couldn't have dinner at home, her mamma would be upset, the only reason she wanted to go to his house just to get to know him a little better. A few days later she seemed not sure where to go to dinner she decided to eat over at his house, but then soon as she got there with the her kids she felt uncomfortable with all the staring. Cheryl finally met Randall's sisters Kim and Judy. Kim seemed friendly but Judy glanced over at her with a mean smirk on her face, as though she was saying what you are doing here. Why are you with my brother? Cheryl notice then we weren't going to be friends she care not to say a word to her. She had to tell him about his sister look. Cheryl she's always been snobbish. Well I feel uncomfortable around her, I think it's better for me and my kids to go back home before I show my ignorance. Calm down Cheryl he said in such a low tone of voice. Cheryl then went onto the porch to release herself Judy wasn't the only one acting snobbish his grandmother was no different, asking the children to sit down and not to move.

She started thinking this wasn't no invitation to dinner it was more like a visit to prison. Dinner was served in a couple of minutes as soon as they ate everybody started to cit chat about death, a discussion she preferred not to engage in. then Cheryl got the kids, Randall it's time for me and the kids to leave it's getting late. Why? We have not had desert yet, we'll get some when I get home. Don't you wanna taste my grandmother's fruitcake? No thank you. She hated fruitcake, she love fruit though. He put some in aluminum foil. All right I'll call you on tomorrow after I go up to the school for an interview for a position. Cheryl was so tired of going from job to job and man to man. the next day she went into the office and asked for Mrs. Moore since she was the person Cheryl supposed to see which she was prompt and on time. A lady came from her office with a cheerful smile hello I see you made it. I'm gonna make this interview short and brief, can you start tomorrow? Sure, Cheryl said. Only problem is the Board of Education sends out the checks, the checks come every three weeks for $74.00 is that okay with you? Yes that will be okay. When she got out of the building she couldn't help but to feel sorry for herself.

After getting fired from a somewhat good-paying security job now she's making a lousy $70.00 every three weeks it will have to do until she could get better. Getting welfare ain't the greatest if $140.00 is all that they will have to live off she would be sickin. She thought about working with the children and all after Brian attend the school. All she thought about was $140.00 a month for five days a week, which was underpaid. Cheryl started the next day for nine months until the summer break. Her first day was excited until the students got uncontrollable after time went on. she had no other alternative to work and plus she was receiving monthly assistance from the Government, considering she have to pay her mama rent buy food ,buy Tylanya and Brian clothes and personal items. This began to be a burden Everyday she felt stressed out living with her family it wasn't fun anymore. They used to be so close but then all of them are growin up now, things started to take a turn for the worst. Every time she came home her sister had dope-dealers in the house. People in the neighborhood was playing dice on the front porch. The bad ones wanted to fight, argue, curse, shoot, it was unbearable.

Cheryl was frustrated she spent more and more time over Randall house. It was one particular guy her sister used to sneak in the house to deal drugs; she didn't know why for the life of her no one used drugs in their home why would this be going down? And her mama said not a word to this dangerous activity at times she would sit on the porch just to get some air, and then Neesha's friends would come up and play dice on the front porch they would be in and out of the house all times of the night. They come over and eat it was mainly the groceries Cheryl paid for. Nessha seldom helped their mama with anything all she does is invite undesirables over. Gerry and Shanetta majority of the time they were going to special events like museums skating rinks, and most of all they continue to stay in the books. While Nesha ran the streets most of the time Cheryl would spend time with the kids, reading and working.

One night she was reading a book she couldn't stand all the sounds of the gunfire that was right outside. Cheryl looked over and her children sleeping through all this turmoil she went over to the window and peeked out of her red-raggedy shades she had up. She didn't look to where someone would notice her there she saw a young guy running up the walkway holding his chest from a gunshot, from that moment she knew she had to leave her parents house it was time to get her own apartment. anyway she 20 years old now it's too much animosity going on in here she can't sleep, the kids have been sleeping with me ever since they were born for the next couple of days they stayed over Randall 's house which she was very much welcomed there Since Judy didn't stay there.

One evening Cheryl decided to go back home where she belong this was the worst day in her life, as she approached the steps her neighbor Lisa pushed her into the concrete. As she got herself up off the ground she asked her what was that about? You know what it's about "Bitch" you have been talking about me she said in a rage. Lisa I have no idea what you are talking about Cheryl said. Not realizing she had a hammer in her hand. There she reached up and clocked her against her hand, and then they got into a brawl. Hours later the cops came speeding up the street then Cheryl was arrested for committing bodily harm. As she tried to explain to them she was pushed down. She consider this to be self-defense. Since Lisa was bleeding from her ear where Cheryl hit her. This was an embarrassment to Cheryl's children and her family as they threw her in the paddy-wagon there she felt like committing suicide. They never told her where she was going when they stopped she looked up to see where she was going. Cheryl couldn't move since they had her tied up like a criminal. She was then taken to a psycho -ward where she was restrained for 19 hours. A couple of hours later she was released on being mentally disturbed. No one picked her up so she had to walk eight blocks to Randall's house. Which he was happy to see her. What happened? It's a long story, and I care not to explain. I wanna hear it. I got into a fight with my neighbor. Look at your face. Yeh she hit me with a mop stick with nails in it, and I hit her with a hammer. But she started the whole commotion. Cheryl didn't want him to see her like this but she had no other choice. She had no money to go home and the hospital was near by where he lived.

She felt humiliated she decided to take a walk as she got to a bridge she stood there for a while wanting to take a dive, that was not a wise decision at that time. Cheryl lost her self-esteem along with dignity she couldn't go back to his house. When she turned around he was standing near her wanting to know what the hell was she was doing. It must didn't cross his mind at that point that I was trying to commit suicide. She thought who would love my children? Who would take them in? Nobody was worth the pain. Life can't be that awful, no it's just some of the people that are corrupted. As I looked over at him with a sadden look on his face shaking his head are you crazy are you out of your mind? What was she doing she thought life is precious to think such fatuous. When he walked back to the house he shouted, she had never saw him in such a rage. "I'm taking you home deal with your own problems I have enough of my own". Shortly they got into his grandfathers old station wagon and he sped off. the next day she got up and knew it was time to get her own apartment, the little money she had wasn't enough to pay bills not only that but to pay all that rent. Word got out if you get into a shelter you will get a place much faster, so she prepared herself and the kids to go sign up when she arrived there was people standing in line waiting to be placed in temporary housing so they call it. some had seats some didn't she didn't mind the wait as long as they get placed and now she can get away from that corrupted neighborhood.

Soon Cheryl's number was called and they told her to report to 1400 Chaplin St N.W. where it was an apartment building turned into temporary housing. as some of the people got up to get into the van which was the transportation bus, Cheryl started shivering afraid they were going to be living in a complete dump. The way there she shed tears here she am going into a shelter and then she couldn't help but to think about what happened. Her and Lisa fought, two grown women well we wasn't women that night. But that was the past it's time to move ahead as they approached the building some of the people were making a lot of unnecessary noise. The room was unbelievable it was a small room with a small dining room table with four chairs in the kitchen. The bathroom was absolutely clean with wall to wall carpeting as well. This is our home for right now she told the kids as they jumped up it's only temporary she said with a bit of relief. They only had time to put their belongings down before they had to go eat at this church, which was not far from the building. there they stood in line to something to eat they served fish patties, mashed potatoes with gravy and green peas Cheryl sat and watched Tylanya and Brian eat thinking to herself it's going to get better, nothing stays the same. It was time for them to return back to TLC that was the name they called it the whole evening.

Cheryl stared out of the window around 9:30 she put the kids to bed she couldn't sleep and got a glass of water. She went to the fringe but nothing was there. Until she gets her food stamps tomorrow, she tried to lay down once again but it was too hot. It was still September and the intense heat began to unbearable so she cut on the air conditioner thank goodness for that. Before she laid down for the third time she got on her knees and thanked the Lord for blessing them. That morning the kids and Cheryl walked up to the grocery store, there was a Giant food store just a couple blocks away she spent over $150,00 on groceries the trip back to the shelter was a climb since they had nine bags of food she carried seven and gave the kids one each. She then fixed some home-made spaghetti the way her mama made it speaking of her mama she forgot to call her. She know she's worried out of her mind. She wanted to call Randall and tell him where they are. It was convenient to have phone booths in the hallways near the elevators on each floor. She called her ma. Where are you I haven't heard from you in three days the children? We're fine we went into a shelter I have my own key to get in and out. "What are the features "? I have a fully remodeled kitchen a clean bathroom, two bedrooms and one coat closet Cheryl said. I'm glad to hear you and my grandchildren are doing fine. Oh I have to hang up they have to room check. Oh before we hang up we have to be in here before 11:00 pm when the counselors come up everybody rushes back into their unit.

Cheryl didn't know anybody there some of them were on drugs, you could tell by looking at some of them. One lady named Shawn down the hall she had five children, Cheryl and her started talking about how nice the shelter was but then she was there for eight months already. She told Cheryl about some of the sneaky and manipulates things going on in the building. Cheryl's mouth hung open when she told her some of the girls there were sleeping with the male counselors just to get an apartment, and then they sneak out of the window to purchase cocaine. What happens if they are caught Cheryl asked they would be put on restriction and wont be allowed to go out for 30 days. I guess that's rough on them. So Shawn if you been in here for eight months are you getting any feedback on an apartment. No not yet I will have to meet with the housing authority, I hope I won't be in here too much longer and don't think it's easy she told Cheryl, with a disappointing look on her face. The only thing she would have to get use to is to be back at a certain time. She would just have to get use to it .she been here so damn long talking to her made her feel much better. She know she can be confident and go through with this day to day went by it was going on two months Cheryl been here she then began to get impatient. That night she called Randall to let him know where she was living hearing his voice she wasn't sure he was happy to hear from her. She guesses he was much too upset with her when she tried to hurt herself a month ago. Maybe he's interested in someone else she began having some feelings for him. She stopped calling for awhile, and months went by before she knew it she was there for four months.

Cheryl was pulling her hair she was frustrated wondering when she was leaving this place one day everybody had to leave the building; someone had pulled the fire alarm. They didn't see a fire until they got on the fourth floor flaming once everybody went outside of the building. This guy walked up and asked if Cheryl washed her face this morning? She thought this place is for women and children, she said to him what are you doing in here in the first place? It was none of my business he said. After the fire engine came and the causes was over Cheryl starting asking questions about this bum. A lady on the third floor was telling her that he was nothing but a whore, it's just him and his daughter he's fucking everybody in the building. Sharon said he has no job he had the nerve to walk up to me and said did I wash my face Cheryl said. Oh that was to see if he can get in your underwear. I advise he keep sleeping with them. He won't have a chance with me girl. These women will fight over this dude Earl.

After talking to Sharon, Cheryl went back into her apartment where she belongs. A couple days later she had to work not only that she did some job hunting. getting back everybody was sitting in the hallway gossiping about people which Cheryl did hear her name and that guy Earl but she kept walking to her apartment she really didn't feel like anything as tired as she was. If every I leave this place she thought. at 6:15 in the morning Cheryl gets up and dress herself Tylanya and Brian traveling on the other side of town take Tylanya over to her mama's and her and Brian off to Fletcher Johnson. On days that she don't have to work she's job hunting or looking for permanent housing. Some of these women love living here they have no rent to pay no furniture to buy. No type of responsibility at all. The only thing they have to do is to answer to somebody and obey the rules and regulations. Which Cheryl did what she suppose to do. Later that evening that guy Earl knocked on her door to borrow some sugar. Days after that they became buddies so a couple weeks later word got out that Shawn was moving out everybody got together and gave her a going away party. The night of the party one of the counselors said it was okay. the party was nice people was drinking alcohol beverages which they sneaked in. during the party Earl announced his family was giving a house party and wanted them to show up.

as Cheryl sat down in the chair Mr. Minor was the counselor there he was staring at Cheryl, he finally came over where she was sitting she was hoping he wouldn't see them with that liquor and then he whispered in her ear saying I would love to kiss you all over. A week later Mr. Minor and Cheryl made love she didn't feel bad about that because she needed some attention. Cheryl haven't seen him in over two months she forgot all about him as she started sleeping around with Marvin. Until one day he finally called and left a message with her mom saying he misses her and please call. Cheryl wasn't too exited about the message he left, he wasn't happy to hear from her. She took her time to call him back. Time was coming closer she was having fun some days and some were dreadful. Mr. Minor would take her out some days. Cheryl felt scared for him since he was the counselor and all but she sure he knew what he was doing that day. That evening Earl knocked on her door to borrow some flour, she let him in, the smell from the alcohol was unbearable. For some odd reason, he made himself comfortable in the dining room area. Is it okay if I sit here and listen to some music it's fine with you?

A few minutes there was a knock on the door when I opened it, Pearl from the third floor telling Earl to get his ass back to his apartment. As she barged her way through Cheryl apartment but Earl sat there with this strange look on his face. After she left in a rage he propositioned Cheryl by stripping down to barely nothing. She couldn't say a word but take off and run told him to leave. By morning she was still in shock she thought about it he must have been sleeping with Pearl. She wasn't interested in him, so she wasn't bothered. the first of the month and everybody was smiling rushing downstairs to get their checks some of them had to go H sty N. E to get them including Cheryl there was a long line people waiting for their Government funds food, help, Cheryl was embarrassed waiting in line herself, all of them needed help to be able to support their families. Cheryl got to the front of the line she had some other mail a letter from the Housing Authority saying she got an apartment at Potomac Gardens Apartments.

Cheryl thought to herself as bad as she wanted to get out of the shelter but she refused to move in those deteriorated projects. A month later she saw some names on the board, and her name was on the listed. She then received another letter saying that her name has reached the top of the list for a housing certificate, which she was happy about the news. Not long she found an apartment it was located on Labium ST. S. E that night she moved in and Randall came over and spent the night with her. It was exciting having him there with her it was all to excited she was overwhelmed when she realized how spacious the apartment was. Night after night Randall came over at one time she thought for a moment he moved in, he started changing. He stop coming over like he used to, he never kept any money. Cheryl wanted to pry in his business she then called his grandmother to ask some questions. Two weeks went past she heard nothing she began to worry she took a chance to go to his house. Long time no see she told him. What are you doing here? I didn't tell you to come over here he said. As he got closer to her he didn't look like the same person he smelled bad his breath smelled horrible. She didn't say a word except stood there with her mouth hung open she was so unhappy about the way he appeared to her that she broke into tears nothing but sadness. She told him about feeling sorry for him, you looked pitiful. What did you say "bitch"? Since you want to disrespect me come get your pants out of my apartment.

The next thing she knew she was running from Randall house with him chasing her with a butcher knife. From that day she was ashamed of going anywhere covered with bruises, scars, and bloody noses. Deep inside she knew this was the end of the relationship but for some reason she fell in love with him. After she left watching him in that violet rage she didn't bother to call him for a couple days. Later that evening sitting there watching TV she felt good about having her own apartment. There was a knock on the door she got up to look out of the peephole; he was standing there looking pitiful she didn't want to let him in, afraid of what he might do. When she opened the door he barged his way through as though he didn't notice the black bruise under my eye, which he did with his powerful fist. Days later, she felt sick she already missed her menstruation before she made an appointment to see if she was pregnant. The situation she was in she couldn't afford any more children she knew she was having a rough time with the two she had already.

Cheryl needed to give this some thought. Time was running out so she decided to have an abortion this was a harsh decision she concluded. But having a third child she couldn't handle this, God wouldn't forgive her she thought. Cheryl asked for forgiveness before she went in for surgery. She felt worse she was harming a human being. Cheryl shivered all over until she walked in the office. Cheryl the doctor wants to see you now. Plucking the $200.00 she had to pay to harm her own baby. The nurse told Cheryl to relax it will be over soon. In fact according to your vaginal walls you have bruised blood you wouldn't carry this baby full term anyway. No matter what she said this was still wrong in Cheryl's eyes and god's. After the procedure was done she began feeling suicidal again she wanted to call him and tell him what she done but the guilt kept nipping at her. She didn't want to go home at that moment and since the kids were at her mama's house, so she went over there and could barely move the pain was intensifying. She couldn't wait till she sat down by the time she was ready to leave blood starting gushing everywhere.

Cheryl went to the bathroom to pad herself. She got to the bus stop two ladies were standing there staring at me are you okay miss one said? Yes I'm fine what happened the other lady said being nosey they assumed I had surgery. I got an abortion. I 'm sorry about that. Well, it was nice chatting with you ladies my bus is coming. When she got home she was too exhausted to do anything. She couldn't stop thinking about what she did she needed rest. Since the kids were at her mama's she wouldn't get so agitated. As soon as she lied down Randall comes over what took you so long to open the door? I'm sore. From what he said? I had surgery today. What kind of surgery? I had an abortion. What? As he got closer to Cheryl his breath smelled like alcohol. I know you didn't say what I thought you said. Why are you so angry? Cause I can't have no sex. then he knocked Cheryl down on the bare cold floor where she he came behind her, he grabbed her by the hair pulling her into the bedroom saying you dumb monkey-mutherfuckin bitch you killed my baby. I haven't had sex with you in weeks I wanna fuck right now. I can't afford it. So what bitch. You have been drinking. The more she talked the more beatings she got. As she tried to reach for the telephone he knocked it out of her hand and repeatedly stomped on her back several times with his feet.

Cheryl begged him to stop. You know I love beating your ass bitch and right now you deserve it for that stupid move you made. What are you talking? About she could barely move or speak or get up. Cheryl finally raised herself from the floor she told him to leave her apartment. Yeh I'm leaving and I ain't never coming back to this muthinfuckin place no more. Cheryl was angry and hurt she stopped calling him for a month, but then he couldn't stay and after what he did to her. She never could forget, two months went by and they made up for some reason. She was still upset about the way he abused her and particular on that day she was in so much in pain and suffering. another month went by he was calm and being so nice, one day they got passionate as she watched him put on his clothes he ask is something wrong? No, I'm just pregnant again. I missed my cycle. Isn't it something you want to say since you reacted so violently the last time? You going to have the baby? Yes I am. So you happy about it? Even if it means we have financial problems? We can handle it. And sure enough her test came back positive. She was kinda upset about being pregnant cause she couldn't afford another baby.

Sitting on the porch there was a guy staring at her from the top of the stairs in the building Cheryl lived in was four unit apartment. He then introduced himself to Cheryl saying his name is Tim he looked sort of weird and as days and months went by he started causing conflict. Then she thought she had the neighbor from hell. She tried to ignore him sometimes but he made it obvious to bother her. She mainly concentrated on her relationship with her kids and Randall. Cheryl was happy with Randall. He even watched Tylanya and Brian awhile she attended child birth classes. She was excited about going because it gave a chance to learn new things certain she never knew about being a parent.

Considering she had three children now at the age of 22. It was Valentines Day and it was her mama's birthday she wanted to buy her something nice for her birthday. She saved $270.00 the day she went to lamas class he babysitted for her while she attended which he normally does when they have class.

When she returned the money she was saving some was missing. Cheryl looked all over the apartment to make sure she didn't misplace it. She was sure she put it in her holy bible her last notion. She knew he stole her money. Part of that money was for my mother's birthday gift she said. Yeh I took it. What did you do with it? Don't ask me nothing stupid bitch I smoked crack with it. Cheryl got so angry when she heard him speak of drugs. Get out get out I said. If you let me explain. Get yourself out the door she said. I ain't going no damn where. Alright I'm leaving then. She slammed the front door after he left she didn't bother to call him. She was threw with this rat race. Two weeks later she met this guy named Brandon but then she knew she couldn't date him considering her condition.

Cheryl invited him over for dinner and he accepted she wanted to tell him about her pregnancy. Three weeks later they ended up in bed and that's when she told him. Are you having the baby? Yes I am she said. Ok it's your decision. But telling him didn't change anything. He stopped calling or coming over she wanted to know where he was. She then gave up searching for him she stood there by the window watching the wind blow from the outside with the curtains pulled back with tears rolling down her face. Cheryl felt sorry for herself she wanted to call Randall but her pride got in the way.

The phone rang she picked it up. It's me Randall look Cheryl I have a drug problem I'm quite sure you know about that. Yes I'm aware of that, how did you start substance abuse? When I was in the Service. Maybe we should break up he said. What about the baby just find somebody else? I don't want anybody else I love you too much. Well can you come over today? Maybe next week I'm going into the Veteran's Hospital for Drug treatment. When are you leaving in three weeks? I'll call you later. Cheryl was now in her third month of pregnancy she was feeling energized more carefree. A month later he went in for help while he was away she felt better about herself. She met her other neighbor Angela she was nice, but Tim was the neighbor from hell he was gay and kept confusion going. One day she was playing some music and the police came banging on the door telling her to turn the volume down.

Another incident she gave a party at her apartment by then Randall returned from the drug treatment and some of the people she met in the shelter were invited. Earl and his family came over to the party turned out really nice except for Tim causing conflict. Again in the middle of the party the police arrived and asked her to turn down the music then a second call was made warning her for the last time by then. Cheryl was angry turn the music back on so that it won't be anymore confusion. The next day there was a hole in the door it was no guessing who did it, because she knew Tim did this. For the next couple of weeks Cheryl began searching for another apartment Randall and her started arguing and fighting again so he returned back to the treatment center now she's hoping to end this relationship. Nevertheless to get away from him and that mean hateful neighbor that lives upstairs. when tried to ignore Randall but he just kept calling me, once she told him she was thinking about relocating to another area, the only reason is because Tim is so much of a trouble maker and she will never have any peace living here. After she hung up from Randall she saw Tim in the hallway actually he listening to her door with his earlobe pressed against the door. She asked him what was he doing and why did he bang a hole in her door that's destruction of property, and he said he felt like it he told her he hit it with a hammer.

Then he pushed her out onto the porch where Cheryl fell down on her knees and scraped her elbow. She knew she had to leave; the police sped up the street at which he called the police on her whereas he put his hands on her. When they arrived she told them he put his hands on her and put a hole in her door. They didn't even arrest him for assault they told Cheryl to get a restraining order against him, where as he's living upstairs. Randall called again and she told what happened and he acted as though he didn't care what Tim did to her. We couldn't even have a pleasant conversation without arguing over the phone bitch, he said. That's all I was to him she thought, so Cheryl wanted revenge by calling the treatment center and telling the drug counselors that they are wasting tax payers money to support those drug addicts. Somehow he received the message that Cheryl was making phone calls at which she didn't care what he thought or said to her. By that time she was preparing herself to move into a much larger apartment, on March 3, 1993 to a three bedroom two full bath.

At five months pregnant no job and a little money from the Welfare department things couldn't get any worse. On top of it all their relationship was going down hill she had no where else to turn by the end of March she was already settled in. He came back from the program knocking at the door with a sad look upon his face. Well are you going to say something? No why the fuck you call the center and tell that bullshit. Just to get back at you for what you put me through. That was no damn reason to call there. Cheryl was upset, later on that night he didn't even tried to touch her which made her angrier. When she reached up to caress him he grabbed his belt from his pants he was wearing and swapped her with it across her face. With her bulging belly the next morning Cheryl looked at herself in the mirror. Her face was swollen, with bruises, cuts and her stomach was bleeding she felt terrible and she looked horrible. She was afraid of him of what he might do or if someone will read about her in the metro section in the Washington Post. He said nothing, no apologies Cheryl suppose he wanted her to apologize as he gazed over at her with a sly grin on his face, saying you look fucked up bitch. Cheryl was now in eight month of pregnancy and she still wasn't happy. Having Randall in her life day by day the situation didn't get any better.

On a bright sunny day he went over to his grandma's house to help out with the garden when he got back he brought back a black cat. Cheryl assumed he wanted the cat there in the house and having a cat wasn't a good idea since she's still pregnant. I don't think you should have brought that cat here Cheryl said. Don't tell me what to do fat-ass monkey mutheerfuckin bitch, move out of way. As he grabbed Cheryl by the arm and yanked her away from the front door as she tried to throw the cat out the door. That same evening two of her friends came to visit Vera and Delonda. He acted like a complete fool he told them to leave so he can finish his violet acts.

One week later Cheryl went into labor around 2:30 am, she felt a bit of discomfort so Randall called his grandmother and grandfather to pick them up to go the hospital. Cheryl had no chose but to go Columbia Hospital for women. There wasn't that much time left before she was rolled into the delivery room. Where the doctor had to perform a caesarian section since the baby was in a breech position. A couple hours later her son was born weighing 11lbs and 6ozs. The surgery made her a little sore and exhausted. Her stay at the hospital was delayed since her son was transferred to the intensive care unit because of his weight. Cheryl decided to name him Terrance, since she would be discharged in four days. The day she was discharged her mama came to give her a ride, as she was rolled downstairs into the lobby area she kept kissing his smooth tender skin.

When she got home Randall did most of the chores all she did was rest and fed Terrance. At night they both would take turns waking up through the night to give him his feedings. Everything seemed to be going fine as long as he wouldn't turn into Dr, Jekyll. Until one day a couple of her friends, Angela and Jimmy wanted to stop over. Randall started a new job as he entered the house they were all sitting in the living room enjoying their selves but Randall just spoke and went to the back. So Cheryl followed him back there to assist him with his clothing, which appeared to be a little babyish he reached up and hit her in the mouth with his fist several times. She couldn't do anything but run from the house with a look of embarrassment. She wanted to call the police but she didn't want to wake up the kids, after the humiliation Angela and jimmy left. For the next few days she walked around the apartment with a swollen lip barely could speak nor talk half of the time.

Cheryl stayed in her bedroom she couldn't explain to her kids what happened she notice the glance they gave her. Terrance was just an infant but Tylanya and Brian were old enough to understand that she was in pain. Cheryl couldn't stand to see him walking around as though nothing happened. She knew it was time to end this horrible so-called relationship but she was afraid of him. He left to get a beer and she was relieved when he came back she could tell from the smell from his breath he not only had beer but alcohol. She knew the drinking was going to create confusion, at the end of the day his attitude got more violent. His voice got louder it was nothing she could do as she was closing her bedroom door to keep from seeing his temper flare which most of the time it did the kids begin to cry in the other room. she wanted to go in their room to calm them down and tell them everything is going to be okay, but as she attempt to go in their room he grabbed her by the hair slapping and punching her over and over in the face. He finally calms down and she breathed sigh of relief he began pacing the floor as if he wasn't finish growling.

Cheryl finally tried to lie down and get some rest since she was bruised so it was a bit uncomfortable, however the peace didn't last long. Cheryl, he kept saying wake up will you let me do something he said. What? She was thinking he wanted to have sex with her, the way he's been acting of course the answer would be no she thought. I want to fuck. No I'm not having sex with you. You're telling me no "bitch". Yes I am I can't take your violent explosions she said. As she attempt to get away from him he grabbed her and pushed her down on the bed and grabbed both her legs and roughly pushed a screwdriver into her vagina this was a nightmare as she stood there bleeding from genital area. She was immediately rushed to the nearest hospital lying there in pain tears was rolling down her cheeks. She couldn't move the doctor finally examined her and said that she had a chronic case of gonorrhea and the tool used ruptured her uterus. When she was released she had to stay on bed rest for three weeks.

Cheryl didn't know how she was going to get around and she had to go to the grocery store because her food was getting low and Randall took some food and stole some money from her. Now that he's gone which he left a couple days after the incident? After she recovered she had to find a way to get back at him for all the turmoil he put her through. One day she got dressed in the shortest dress she could find to stand on the side of the street, hoping no one would think she prostituting. Which she wasn't. Cheryl turned to go back in the house noticing she was making a fool out of myself. A burgundy –caravan pulls up and a man gets out and says hello I'm drew and you are? I'm Cheryl. She knew what was going to happen just sex. A week went pass and drew and her spent a lot of time together. Not looking for a relationship all she wanted to do is get back at Randall. The next week she had sex with Drew on her living room floor after she put the kids to bed. She was wishing Randall won't show up. Cheryl didn't want to take advantage of Drew but she wasn't looking for love either. As time went by Drew stop coming over so often cause she told him about her situation.

Then one day he came to take Cheryl and the kids to Chuck cheese a place where they serve pizza and have children's rides. Which the kids enjoyed themselves and so did she. The next couple of days Randall showed up intoxicated and drugged out of his mind. Cheryl knew when she let him in he was going to cause trouble; she only did it on the strength of Terrance. Later on that evening Lynn and Rick showed up to visit her and the kids. The phone rang it was Drew on the other end of the phone since Randall was there she went into the bathroom to talk where she can have some privacy. After her conversation with him was over, there was Randall standing at the door listening the entire time. You sneaky-rotten bitch he said. Please don't start we have guests here. I don't give a fuck I overheard you talking to some man. You and I are no longer a couple you treat me like dirt. So what is it to you? I put my mouth on your nasty ass you dirty low down bitch. Go home I don't need it today she said. Listening to his raging temper once again, she tried to walk out of the house as she approached the front door he kept pulling her by the hair beating her constantly with his fist stomping onto her back with the hard combat boots he was wearing. He wouldn't stop until the police department arrived instantly they removed him from the apartment. Easter was coming soon and Cheryl intended on taking the kids to the circus. That came to an end later on that evening he broke into the apartment and stole her brand-new pioneer system she purchased a couple weeks ago. By the time the police came again telling him to leave the premises he resisted that's when they used excessive force on him. Cheryl was glad she could breathe again, for a whole month. Until she decided to take the baby over for a visit with him, as she was leaving he begin punching her in the throat in the middle of 30th street where he lived saying you caused me to get arrested. Cheryl called the police again and they arrived he was immediately arrested on his front porch one officer asked if she wanted to proceed with the charges. Of course, her answer was yes. Terrance was without a father but at least she knew she can show her face again and smile.

Chapter 9

Easy Lay

After two weeks Cheryl brought Terrance over just to see him, which was a dumb move she made. As she got there he was sitting on the front porch with some girl, Cheryl got so angry she threw his clothes into the street he then hit her in the neck and the face. She called the police and the ambulance at which she couldn't move her neck. Cheryl was so embarrassed because of this.

❧ ❧ ❧

The ambulance pulled up in front of Randall house while the police arrested him after he kept beating her in the face with his fist. Shaking as the paramedic gently rolled her in to the wheelchair she couldn't barely move trying to hide her face. There were people standing all around staring at her. When Cheryl arrived at the hospital she sat there for nearly three hours they finally called her name in the triage area. After she was treated and waiting on her results from the x-ray she also had to get some STD tests done, everything was ok except for having a slight yeast infection. Leaving the emergency room the security guy asked Cheryl what happen to her face, she didn't want to tell him her business. I see you have on a neck brace he said. Since you wanna know I was beaten by an ex-boyfriend she said. He did a job on you. Then let that be the reason I got rid of him. Damn that's fucked up. Listen I don't have to explain nothing to you. I'm just concern miss if you need to talk my name is Mack here's my phone number call me ok. That's not necessary she said harshly as she balled up the piece of paper ramming it into her purse.

Later Cheryl called Mack, hey! Have you calmed down yet he said? Yes I'm just glad this is all over and I can get on with a normal life. That's what it's all about taking care of yourself he said. I should have been taking care of me from the start. You mind me asking you something. No go ahead. How long have you two been together four long miserable years the whole time he's using drugs. What kind of drugs? Cocaine that I knew of. I guess that's what changed his attitude at times he was sweet, kind and loving and the other times he was mean, and brutal. I 'm relieved and now can take a breath of fresh air. I was blind and couldn't see how I couldn't predict the way the relationship would be. Actually, what he taken you through there's no chance for anybody else now. I'm not going to say that maybe one day I'll find the person I'm compatible with. I'm at peace right now with my life. I had a brother that used drugs and died from an overdose of heroin our entire family was destroyed over that. It's not a good feeling. Well, Cheryl I have rounds to do.

After that they said their goodbyes and they hung up the phone. A week later he came over and they had a couple of beers which Cheryl wasn't a beer drinker. He started to touch her on her breast, his touching begin to be unbearable but she had to be strong she was still in pain. All she knew was he wanted her for sex she had asked him to leave. Father's day was approaching and she went out to buy Mack a shirt with blue and white prints on it. When he came over smiling as usual. I have something for you she said. Thank you, but it's too big. Take it back. Cheryl sat there feeling bad and staring at him feeling embarrassed about the shirt he didn't want it. It was going on 3:00 in the morning and he had to leave as soon as they had sex. The next day she didn't bother to call him after all he knew what state of mind she was in; he was taking advantage of her so she won't call him unless he calls her. Two days later he comes over as she went over to open the door for him, hey Cheryl can you loan me $20.00 for my cleaners I need to get my uniforms out he said. Sure, reaching down into her pocketbook to hand him the money. Thanks I'll give it back tomorrow. Sure you will in a sarcastic manner she said. Mack why is it the only times I talk to you it's at the hospital? Because I don't have a home phone. Okay I have a girlfriend and she's pregnant. There's so much to tell. Ok I 'm still married to my wife. You're telling me you're involved with three women? No just two, you and me just sleep together, he said meaning it. Since you said it like that we can stop seeing each other right now.

No I didn't mean it like that. What did you mean? You just got out of a relationship and I'm still involved, we can't establish anything. You're right, but since you only have room for two women in your life seeing another won't make matter any easier, and I'm not to allow you to dig in the cookie jar whereas you just had ice cream and cake after The petty discussion they had made they ended up in bed anyway Cheryl was still empty after it was all over.

This time Cheryl notice something, there were tiny bumps on the edge of his penis. What is this she asks? Oh I was diagnosed with herpes simplex years ago. Why didn't you tell me in the beginning? I was gonna tell you, I was waiting on the right time. You found the time to get me in bed. You gonna past this infection on without telling me? Why are you worrying I had on a condom? You're infected! I was going to tell you, stop yelling! Where are you going? He got up and put on his pants and shirt he left. The next day he called to apologize about last night. Cheryl on her way to the clinic on Banning Rd, she waited four hours for her results, and they finally let her know she don't have no signs of Herpes. Cheryl has not spoken with him in two weeks when she did he asked can he come over. No she said go home with your pregnant girlfriend! She angry about what he told her. You should have told me, you should have been honest. I wasn't what's the big fuckin deal? I tell you what go tell your girlfriend and see if it's a big fuckin deal to her. If that's the way you want it then I'm gone he said.

A few hours later he came over with a guilty look on his face, wishing he didn't say those things to her.

Every time they would try to talk it over they could never see anything eye to eye. Cheryl knew this was not a relationship it was bed after bed every other night. She allowed this happen and knew some time soon she had to end this bed sweat, cause that's all it was. They both knew they couldn't continue on with this fling. As they laid in the bed for 1000th time this was not heading nowhere. She was perfect for him but he wasn't for her for the last time he walked out of her door. For three weeks she hasn't heard from him. A month later she got a call from Earl from the shelter, he was incarcerated for violating his parole. It was nice to hear from him as they went on and on about the parties and all the commotion that went on at TLC where they all had some good times and some bad ones too. Cheryl enjoyed talking to Earl, but she got a deep pain in her stomach thinking about Mack. Day in day out made Cheryl sick; she had to stop thinking about him he loved two women and not three. Now she strongly believe just because someone give themselves to you, don't mean they love and want to be with you.

CHAPTER 10

Disappointed

Cheryl barely got out of the shower good, before she heard a knock at the door. When she went to open the door, it was Earl from the shelter standing there with a black bag in his hand along with his brother-in law Redds. It was a surprise to see him since she haven't seen him in two years all she could see was that gold tooth he had grinning. Giving her a big hug as though he was trying to give a hint. I ain't seen you in a long time he said. But they talked over the phone. Whatcha been up to? Nothing just trying to stay out of trouble. You better. Being in the penitentiary ain't no joke man, fuckin around with them bamms got me in trouble. No you got yourself in trouble. She told him with a strong look on her face.

So tell me you and Randall still together? No that man, drove me into the fire and back and I'm more complete with myself and inner feelings. Basically, I'm just resting and getting my thoughts together. How is those daughters of yours and your other half? Who? Aileen. Oh she's locked up now. For what? Some bullshit, we're not together anyway I'm just chilling right now. Do you remember what I used to ask you? No. pretending like she didn't realize what he was talking about. While we were living in the TLC shelter. Cheryl knew he was attracted to her then and now but she wasn't attracted to him. Have you refreshened your mind yet? Are you crazy, no I'm not letting you have oral sex on me? Why not? It wouldn't be appropriate. Cheryl you know I had a crush on you. I know you did but you slept with a lot of women in the building the word went around that you were the male whore. I wasn't involved with anybody then I was a single man that's what single men do. Oh! Back to what you asked me that's the reason because of your male ego. You're my best friend and I don't want to ruin our relationship by sleeping with you. I like you as a friend but not as a lover. Can we talk about it? First of all, you are the kind of person that can't be loyal, even if you were in a relationship.

Being locked up made me wake up. Let's change the subject Earl. Okay. When is the next party well? Actually since you're out of jail we can arrange something. Like what? Joking as he normally does a party silly! So it will be a welcome home party. Let's go in your bedroom. I told you I'm not sleeping with you Earl. As she turned around and it was non-stop kissing and then there they were, she was embarrassed for what she did.

Once again Cheryl allowed her hungry flesh take over her mind and how she felt. Especially after knowing how many women he has been with. She knew when Shawn finds out she's going to be hysterical, even though when she was in TLC Earl was her secret lover. Cause she has a boyfriend at that time she said she wasn't in involved with Earl. Cheryl confronted her about it. Two weeks later they had the party for him it went well it was a couple of fights occurred Cheryl wasn't sure that she wanted to give the party or not considering how everybody going to think why is she giving him a party of all people and he's not her boyfriend. She didn't care after the party was over he kept hanging around her apartment pretending as if he was catching a taxi cab.

She knew what he was really up to and then lying to Shawn about it. Cheryl was sure she knew what he was up to, they went into the bedroom and she kept asking herself, why are you doing this, just to please your pleasures because your sex drive is high? You just have to have a man in your life even if they are not up to your expectations, they can't help me financially she thought? After everybody left they went into the bedroom and they had sex and she felt guilty afterwards. Not just about the sex but it wasn't exciting. The next day Cheryl received threatening phone calls from Shawn saying she's nothing but a low down dirty slut in such an angry voice. Listen Shawn you told me and everybody that you and Earl had no connections and he also said there was nothing. Anyway you and Scott are together so how can you call me with this immaturity. I don't care. I never wanna say anything else to you Bitch!

As Cheryl thought about it they shouldn't be sleeping together considering their friendship when she finally called Earl about ending this so-called fling he went on about he and Shawn wasn't never close, but Cheryl couldn't linger this on. Thinking about all those women he slept with in the shelter which you knew this from the beginning. That night Cheryl called his sister Cindy who therefore, gave her some advice she and Shawn were somewhat close. Hello she said. What's up Cheryl? I 'm a little upset that's all. For what? Shawn found out that me and Earl is seeing each other. Well, she was your friend and a lay in the bed isn't worth losing your friendship with somebody. We spoke when we were in the shelter but never close friends, but Earl said he never slept with her. Earl lying she gave him money whenever he asked for it, really? The only reason she did that because Earl has a drug-problem. He had it for a long time. I know. I would end this mess I just got out of a relationship similar to that; I can't bare another unreasonable situation. I like Earl as a friend that's it no more than that. Thanks for telling me. Okay I'll be talking to you she said. The next weekend Cheryl and the kids were invited over to his apartment and of course she accepted. She only came cause she wanted to tell him this can't go on no more. She feel as though he pressed her into this and she was not ready she learning her lesson from her past experiences.

Coming there was the worst weekend she ever had she never knew how his attitude could be. On the other hand she knew about his drug- habit how can she get out of this after all the turmoil and pain she been through. She was starting this all over again all night long he was back and forth out of the apartment this only made her upset because she knew what he was doing. Cheryl had to take a deep breath to keep from hyperventilating the last time he came in he started yelling sayin give me some money dripping with sweat from his body. I don't have any money she said. Stop lying Bitch! Why are calling me names? How did you get over here if you don't have any money? Get out! I'll be glad to let me wake up my children. No they can stay you can leave. As she went into his daughter's room to wake them, he grabbed her by her hair telling her leave bitch! She went into the hallway to get some air and keep from going outside to pick up something to hit him with. She knew she wasn't going no where without her kids. She then heard his raggedy door opening, look right now I ain't mean to say those cruel things about you, will you come inside? I'll come back but I wont accept your apology and in the morning me and my kids are going home. It's bad enough you're in and out of here. Look this is my place I can go as I please. That's why it's a mistake for us to come here. Better yet why won't you leave? I NEED SOME FUCKIN MONEY! When I leave you will never have to worry about me again she said. The next morning they left to go home hoping he wont dial her damn number again. As soon as she gets into the house the phone rang she wanted to answer but she knew it was him.

Cheryl had to build her strength so she picked up the phone cause she got tired of hearing it rang. As she answered he said just listen saying he's sorry I had a few drinks that night and I flipped out so don't shut me out of your life. You're not in my life this was a mistake, so don't tell me that stupid shit. Please please I need you. I don't want any hard feelings between us. As you knew Thanksgiving is two weeks away what are you planning to do? My mother is having dinner at her house. Can't you take a rain-check? Since I been locked up I ain't did nothing. Okay I'll call my mother and tell her we will have dinner with you and your family. I hope she wont be upset. When Cheryl talked to her mama, she seemed mad about the situation. After she hung up she felt bad all this time she had been coming over for Holidays, now all of a sudden she give into a man she barely have feelings for. Knowing her mama she knew that's what exactly what she would thinking, she always thought Cheryl made bad choices in men from the beginning. Which she did. Cheryl didn't know what else to do she wanted to cancel going over there. Two weeks later they all gathered over to his house the whole family stuffing their faces with Turkey, ham, potato salad and six sweet potato pies, collard greens, cakes and all sorts of desserts they had made. It's official about their relationship as she looked around to notice his family, wishing her family was as close. She wouldn't mind marrying into this family. Only if he could change his attitude everybody had taken to her from the start. Especially his mother she was a sweet lady always smiled and helped others when they need it. From that day they all was always together and did things together

Christmas came Cheryl favorite holiday she loved the idea of shopping for the kids watching them waking up in the morning dashing to the Christmas tree that made her happy. Earl and Cheryl were calling each other every day telling each other how much they missed each other. When New Years came the family got together again this time it was over his sister Yvette house her were twins, no one cared too much about Yvette the family said a lot of negative things about her such as she brags a lot and even talking bad about her twin sister. all because of her being an ex- drug addict and all as what Cheryl can see Cindy seemed to be a nice person she taken to her more. So After New Years came in which it was 1996 things had begin to fall apart for the Jones family the closeness they had fallen apart. The laughter, and the talking and getting together had no longer existed. It started when Cindy contacted the HIV virus they tried to keep the disease a secret but Yvette started telling other people, she even confided in Cheryl but she told no one. She wasn't family although she had a relationship with her brother. The next couple of days her illness took a turn for the worst she was admitted in to the hospital for pneumonia the family was worried. Cheryl was worried for her. She enjoyed being around her listening to her making Cheryl laugh giving her advise about certain issues. It was September of that year and she continue to get sick over and over again.

They all went to visit her but she unconscious so they sat around and watched her sleep so peacefully. As soon as they got back to Cheryl's apartment, Yvette got a call from the hospital that Cindy went from HIV to full blown AIDS. Yvette came over when Cheryl opened the door she was crying so bad. No one knew what to do Cheryl was in shock and Earl fell to the floor tears falling from his eyes. Cheryl wanted to grab him and tell him it's going to be okay but she couldn't find the words to tell him. This was his sister and he was going to miss her. Everybody will miss her it was a sad time for the entire family. A couple of days went by and they went to the funeral. A lot of friends of her there crying and saying how much they will miss her. Cheryl never thought this would happen even before her and Earl begin to date she was a nice and outgoing person. After the funeral she was buried, which was much more heart breaking. Cheryl know no one would ever get over her death. A week later Cheryl the kids, and Earl went over to her mama's house to visit, since she haven't been over in a while. She seemed to be excited to see us. But Cheryl noticed that mean streak she had spread over her face towards Earl, and glancing over at her.

Cheryl knew why she gave him that stare, thinking he was the cause why they haven't been over for special occasions. All awhile they were sitting there laughing and joking with one another Cheryl saw how much liquor he was drinking, which made her feel uneasy because she didn't know how he going to react after guzzling glass after glass. Leaving her ma's house Earl was so intoxicated he could hardly stand up, falling to his knees foaming from his mouth cursing Cheryl was afraid of what he might do. As she got out of the car he began to push her unto the ground and hitting her in her face with his fist all because she didn't want to leave her cassette tapes in his car due to the broken lock that was on the passenger side. Cheryl tried to calm him down even begging him to stop beating her and then she lost her balance and fell to the ground and he started kicking her in the face. Pushing her head towards the dashboard and as she ran from him he caught her and consistently kept hitting her in the face with his fist. There was thunderstorms and raining so hard she kept falling to her knees. The next day she stayed in the house too embarrassed to show her face in public for at least three months she didn't speak nor call him. By that time frustration was unbearable, Cheryl's feelings and emotions had taken over. So she called him. which he's been calling for the whole three months they were apart.

Cheryl gave in that Saturday and he came over with his two daughters Bonnie and Denise. So they decided to give a cookout at Cheryl's house she prepared some hotdogs, hamburgers, seafood salad. Later on he was drinking fussing fighting with Cheryl. She couldn't understand his actions after the last incident they had this time he was like a time bomb ready to explode. It surely was surely humiliating since his mom came over and his sister Yvette. Cheryl called the police this time and they asked him to leave. Another month went by, then Cheryl received a letter from the rental stating she had to vacate the premises. Cheryl knew her world was crumbling down and maybe part of having to leave her apartment was her fault. She spent a lot time trying to maintain a relationship, rather than noticing her son was getting into trouble. Cheryl knew that she took care of her children but maybe she should have paid more attention to what was going on. Two months later they moved to the Oak Town area. Moving there was the worst mistake Cheryl made, considering still involved with Earl she knew should have broken up with him. Now his drug- addiction had taken full effect on her and her belongings was stolen from the apartment. Waking up in the middle of the night she couldn't sleep she had to hide her money. One night Cheryl was asleep and he came in fighting on her. She told him to get the fuck out of her apartment and go to his place. He refused. For some reason it was hard to get rid of him. Six months later her apartment caught on fire from a little girl who was babysitting. Cheryl immediately moved to another apartment in Oak Leaf a month after month things got no better. As soon as she would fall asleep he would sneak out and steal majority of her things.

She knew this was over. He came in after she told him to leave she never wanna see him again. Then he wanted to stay over she turned over and he be lying beside her with two butcher knives in the wall. When Cheryl told him once again to leave she got irate and he then left and climbed through her window with a gasoline jug in his hand saying I'll burn your ass up bitch. Cheryl ran from her apartment to call the police from her neighbor's house but never did. When she got back he was standing in the parking lot she went into her house he came in there and raped her. Cheryl called the police and they arrested him on first degree rape. Cheryl went along with the officers to press charges against him, but they didn't keep him when she returned home she knew this was it. she can never understand why she let herself go through so much agony and with all she went through allowing her sexual organ to make a fool out of her. Reaching out for love but love was invisible.

To all women all over the world that have been in complicated circumstances, you will find your way through. God Bless.

What I can say to this is that the pen has been lifted and the ink is dry.

For seven years, I managed to focus more on my children, myself, God, my job and finally loving myself. I'm more stable, and in love. Comfortable and spiritually and finally meeting a wonderful man. The love of my life, my husband, my friend, my lover, and companion.

Printed in the United States
142232LV00001B/27/P

9 781434 375216